ULTIMATE DILEMMA
FORGIVE ME LORD

a novel by Reign

DREAMS BOOKS
DREAMS PUBLISHING COMPANY
www.dreamspublishishing.com

DREAMS PUBLISHING COMPANY
Post Office Box 4731
Rocky Mount, North Carolina 27803
www.DreamsPublishing.com

Dreams Titles are available at special quantity discounts for bulk purchases for sales promotion, premiums, fund-raising, educational, or institutional use. Special book excerpts or customized printings can also be created to fit specific needs. For details, write to:

Dreams Publishing Company, Post Office Box 4731, Rocky Mount, North Carolina 27803; Attention: Special Sales.

Cover Designed by Nicki Angela

ISBN 978-0-9788977-2-7

Library of Congress Control Number (LCCN): 2009920501
1. Family & Relationships – Love & Romance
2. African American Women – Fiction
3. Interpersonal Relationships

First Dreams Books Printing: July 2011

10 9 8 7 6 5 4 3 2 1

Manufactured in the United States of America

Dedication

To my mother, Sula Thomas Walker, born April 3, 1934 – died November 11, 2009. I will always remember you as the greatest woman I have ever known.

&

To my father, Eddie Walker Jr., born January 12, 1931 – died December 22, 2009. Together you and Mom raised not only your own children, but other people's too. We loved you most of all because of your selflessness.

.

Acknowledgements

As always, I wish to first thank my Father and my God through Christ Jesus who brought me peace beyond all understanding in a time of great sorrow. I truly found out that "Earth has no sorrow that heaven can not heal."

To all the libraries throughout the United States that have allowed me to visit you, I am grateful and I thank you.

To all the readers in Alabama who asked me to set this story in Birmingham, this one is for you.

To my proofreaders, Teresa Rhodes and Hope Phillips as always your support and care for me are invaluable.

To my husband, Calvin, thanks for asking me every single day, "Did you work on your manuscript today?"

Matthew 18:21-22 (King James Bible)

Then came Peter to him, and said, Lord, how oft shall my brother sin against me, and I forgive him? till seven times?

Jesus saith unto him, I say not unto thee, Until seven times: but, Until seventy times seven.

1 John 5:17 (Amplified Bible)

All wrongdoing is sin, and there is sin which does not [involve] death [that may be repented of and forgiven]

PROLOGUE

"Monique Cheri Anderson, you are going to bust hell wide open! You can't just come between a man and his wife and think God's not gonna take notice! The devil is a crackhead liar if he thinks that I raised you to be a home wrecker, and I know that I certainly didn't raise you to be a ho!" Bernadette Anderson stood over her daughter, wagging her finger in her face. "What happened to your morals, girl?"

Cheri dropped her head. She had grown up in this house. In this kitchen, from this very table, she had learned many of life's lessons from her mother. Bernadette had raised both her daughters here. So far they had turned out well, graduating from college and becoming assets to society. Sandra, seven years older than her sister, first started off as a math teacher at the local high school. After getting her master's degree, she became principal, and now she was dean of student development at the community college. But she was most proud of Monique Cheri, who, at first, could not seem to find her way in the media industry; now she was a local celebrity, anchoring the morning news for channel six in Philadelphia—and she didn't want anything to tarnish her banner accomplishments.

Cheri had always been secretive, but her mother never imagined that her baby girl would turn out to be the mysterious woman having a long-time affair with one of the most prominent pastors in South Jersey.

"What is wrong with you, girl?" Bernadette asked as if trying to make some sense of the whole thing.

Cheri looked up at her mother with pleading eyes, wanting desperately to make her understand. "I love him, Mama."

"You don't know what love is," Bernadette replied between clenched teeth.

Once again, Cheri dropped her gaze to the floor. "I can't help how I feel."

"It's not about what you feel, it's about obeying God. I can't believe Pastor Owens would leave his wife and children, disgracing himself before the Almighty—and for what? Feelings? It's a scandal and a shame. And to think a child that came from my own body has allowed this vile thing to be committed through her." Bernadette, short in stature but large, walked to the kitchen sink, snatched off her apron, and tossed it onto the counter. She weighed over two hundred and fifty pounds and she carried her weight with the appearance of authority. She looked up to the ceiling, searching for the words to say to make her child understand that what she was about to do was not only immoral but selfish. "How can God be pleased with this … this … horrendous thing you speak of doing? It's an abomination to the Lord!"

"Mama, please, just let me explain," Cheri implored.

Her mother either ignored her or simply didn't hear her plea. "Jesus, Lord, what are people going to say? He's supposed to be a man of God, but now I know all the talk about him is true. I know you heard about him being caught at the Red Roof Inn with his secretary, so you know you're not the only one. If he'll leave his wife for you, then you can expect to be the next victim. Do you hear me? You reap what you sow."

"Mama, just give me…"

"I've never seen a farmer plant corn and it come up peas. You reap what you sow, you hear me?"

Cheri didn't say a word to defend her man, even though she knew the real story behind the rumor. The fact of the matter was it was she who had met Pastor Preston Owens at the Red Roof Inn on that now infamous day. After they made love, he had fallen asleep and she quietly left him in the room spitefully taking his clothes with her. She had been angry with him, angry because she wasn't Mrs. Preston Owens. She was also angry because she was a soon to be thirty-one-year-old woman who had never been married and he had denied her something mostly every woman in the world wanted, children. So, on that day, she left the hotel with everything except his shoes. Pastor Owens had to call his secretary to bring him one of the suits he kept at the church. His secretary had been mistaken for the "other woman" when a member from another church saw her leaving the hotel moments before the pastor. It was because of this that the rumor had started, exposing a half-truth.

When Cheri didn't acknowledge she had heard her mother, Bernadette asked with an edge of disgust, "How did you let this happen? That's all I want to know. How in the world did you let this happen?"

"He wasn't married when I met him, Mama. You know that. You said you liked him. You told me he'd make me a good husband."

"Yes, yes, I said that. But I said it when he wasn't married and you and him were single and dating. Now the fact is, he didn't marry you. You should have left him alone, gave him his walking papers when he picked another woman over you. However, you've allowed that man to have his cake and eat it too."

"Mama, you don't understand. Please let me explain. Preston allowed his…"

"No, no, no. I don't want to hear how you let some hypocrite compromise you."

"Then let Preston talk to you. I'm sure you'll see…"

"I don't want to talk to that man. I don't want him in my presence and I certainly don't want him in my home," she hissed.

"What do you want me to do?" Cheri's heart was breaking.

"You tell that man to go home to his wife and children." Her mother wagged her finger two inches from Cheri's face. "If that man didn't respect the vows he made before God and a church full of family and friends, what makes you think he'll be faithful to you when you take vows with him in some judge's chamber?"

Cheri was quiet as she watched her mother move to sit in a chair opposite her at the kitchen table. "So we're supposed to be miserable for the rest of our lives, denying our love for each other?" It was a question she'd asked herself too many times during the past week.

"That's the choice he made when he married his wife over you," her mother finished bitterly.

How many times had Cheri heard her sister Sandra say, "Preston made his own bed hard when he married a woman he didn't love. So you need to leave him alone and let him lay in that hard bed, without you."

"But why should I suffer for one mistake that can be corrected?" she asked, almost in a whisper.

Her mother softened when she heard the pain in her daughter's voice. "Cheri, look at me, sweetie."

Cheri raised her head, blinking back tears as she gazed into her mother's eyes.

"He had a choice and it wasn't you. He must honor the vows he made before God to his wife."

Cheri dropped her head again and for a long time she didn't say a word.

Her mother thought maybe she had finally gotten through to Cheri, but that hopeful moment was short-lived when she heard her reply. "But, Mama, he wants to fix his mistake. He wants to marry me and start again."

Bernadette wrapped her arms around her youngest child. "Oh, baby, I can only imagine how you feel. But you have to move on. Don't let him drag you down along with him."

"But I love him, Mama. I love him."

Bernadette dropped her arms in frustration.

"Be happy for me, Mama. I'm finally going to be with the only man I've ever loved."

Her mother shut her eyes, knowing she had failed to convince her daughter to do what she thought was right. "I can't celebrate this travesty with you. I won't be a part of it, 'cause if I do, I'd be condoning it." Her mother looked at her sternly with a mixture of something she'd never seen in her eyes. "You'll never be recognized as the real wife and no decent Christian community will have him as pastor, knowing what he's done."

Cheri's mind was made up. "It doesn't matter, because I'm marrying him anyway. The Bible says to obey the law of the land and as long as he divorces, he can marry me. The Bible gives clear directions on how to handle a divorce."

Bernadette sighed. "You are your father's child, that's for sure."

"What does Daddy have to do with this?"

Her mother disregarded the question. "You have to know something," she said, and her voice was low and serious. "You have to know that if you do this, then you will no longer be a daughter of mine."

Cheri gasped, her eyes widening in shock. "Mama, you can't mean that!"

"I do mean it. So you hear me and hear me well. If you marry that man, then forget I'm your mother. I never want to see you again and I will pray God has mercy on your soul."

Cheri found the conversation so ridiculous she almost laughed. "I love him, why can't you understand that?"

"You choose this day who you will serve. Your flesh, or the Lord?"

Cheri did not want to lose her mother over this. That would be the ultimate sacrifice.

Bernadette stood up. "Now, if you choose to repent …" She nodded her head a few times. "I'll … I will support you through this whole mess. It will simply be said that the pastor took advantage of you. He was a man of the cloth and you trusted him, and he took advantage of your being naive. I'm sure this can be salvaged for you." She looked at her daughter with a mixture of compassion and sorrow before turning away. "But if you choose to marry that man, then I want you to leave my house and never return, not even when I die."

"Mama…" Cheri's eyes watered. She knew her mother meant what she was saying. Yet she could not understand how she could disown her as if she weren't flesh of her flesh. "Mama, please. You don't know what you're saying."

"Oh, I know exactly what I'm saying. You want to try me? Marry him and see. You will no longer be welcome here. I don't want you contacting me for anything, and I mean that." Her mother stared and shook her head in silence. "You know your way out," Bernadette said and walked out of the kitchen.

Cheri watched as her mother disappeared into the next room. She blew out a long sigh, knowing there was no way to make her understand her point of view. She would need time.

As she walked out the back door to get into her car, she turned to look at the house that held so many memories and wished that things could have been different.

It seemed ironic to Cheri that Luther Ingram's long-ago song, If Loving You Is Wrong, I Don't Want To Be Right, would be playing on the radio as she drove away from her mother's house. What was she to do? Give up the best thing she'd ever had? She loved Preston Owens more than she wanted to, and although she felt deep in her heart that it was wrong, she still needed him like the air she breathed.

And just as the lyrics of the song said, Preston had a wife and two children who all depended on him being a loving husband and father. She was sure the children loved and adored him more than words could ever express with the pure hearts that only a child could give. As for his wife, Nadine, Cheri could only imagine how she felt. Nadine owned the right to have his affection, soft caresses, tender kisses, fiery passion, mixed with an intensity that only true love is able to render.

Yet all of it was given to Cheri.

Cheri pulled into a parking place at the restaurant, leaned back in her seat, and closed her eyes tightly. She was supposed to be meeting Preston there. She thought about everything her mother had said. She knew

Bernadette was right. He would never preach again, at least not in this area. Too many people knew all too well of his infidelity. Taking a deep breath, she went in and saw Preston almost at once. She gave him a weak smile as he stood to pull out her chair and kiss her cheek.

Preston sat down and signaled for the waiter. "I can tell it didn't go well, so … let's eat first and then we'll talk. I'm hungry and I don't want to hear any news to upset my appetite."

Cheri nodded wordlessly. Her mother had made it crystal clear: her, or her man.

Cheri couldn't even think about food. She had to make a decision. Losing her mother meant losing her only sister, too. No one in the family would speak to her again. Her mother had that much power.

"Cheri? Cheri?"

"Yes… Sorry."

"You know what you want?" Preston asked.

"Just a club soda, thanks," Cheri massaged her left temple with her fingertips.

"He's taking your food order, too," Preston said.

She shrugged. "I'm not very hungry, nothing for me."

"What about a slice of cheesecake? It's very good," the waiter suggested.

"No, thanks, just a club soda." Would he never leave?

After the waiter walked away, Preston reached across the table, taking both her hands in his. "It was that bad?"

There were tears pressing against the backs of her eyeballs. "Worse."

He massaged her hands. "You want to talk about it now?"

"No, you're right, you should eat first."

He only made it through about half his meal. Cheri looked miserable. "Tell me what happened," Preston urged.

Cheri paused, then swallowed hard. "I can't marry you, Preston."

"What?" His ears had to be deceiving him.

She looked at him. "I'm sorry, but this just isn't right. We need to go our separate ways. My mother said she'll stand by me—as long as I do what's right."

"I asked you to let me talk to your mother," he reminded her.

"My mother wants nothing to do with you." Cheri stood up. "I'm so sorry. I really didn't want it to be this way, but I can't—I just can't—lose my entire family for a man who ... who may or may not be with me for the rest of my life."

"Sit down, baby."

"I want ..."

"Sit down, now," Preston said sharply.

Cheri stared at him without blinking.

He softened his tone. "Please, Cheri, I need a chance to understand why you've come to this conclusion." When she continued to stare, he added, "I'm begging you."

She sat down silently.

Preston was almost whispering when he said, "I don't know what your mother said to you, but whatever it was, it couldn't have been pretty, I'm sure. I love you, baby. I have always loved you. I messed up. You know it and I know it. Now, please don't turn your back on me now that I've made the ultimate sacrifice."

"What sacrifice is that, Preston? Leaving your wife and children?" She was being sarcastic.

"No. Leaving the church," he answered without hesitation as tears welled in his eyes.

"All I have left is my family." She was hurting too.

He nodded. "And all I have left is you."

"We can't stay in this city. But I know you don't want to leave your children."

"My children won't even speak to me. My parents won't have anything to do with me. The members of the church have turned their backs on me. All I have is you."

Cheri thought for a moment, "God has truly forsaken us. But if we do the right thing and repent, then maybe, just maybe we can be redeemed. I don't want to live in exile, and I'm sure with time …"

He cut her off. "Tell me what your mother said to you."

"You don't want to know." She shivered.

"Yes, I do: tell me." He knew he sounded demanding but he needed to know.

Cheri paused. Did she really need to say all those hateful and hurtful things to him? "I don't want to tell you. She was downright mean."

"Tell me anyway. I'm a big boy."

She told him everything.

"I see. She threatened you by saying she won't speak to you ever again and that's childish, but I understand. She has strong convictions. And she's right about us not being respected here. That's why we're moving to another state. Nobody will know us and we'll have a brand new start."

"I can't just leave my job," Cheri protested. "I worked hard to get that position. And what about my family?"

"We're family now," he said, putting her hand to his lips and kissing her index finger. "Don't abandon me," he said and kissed the next finger. "I don't want to live without you," he added, kissing the next finger. "Don't allow your mother to kill our dreams," he pleaded, kissing her last finger. "Your mother has lived her life, and she can't live yours," he finished, kissing the palm of her hand then pressing it to his face.

He'd already had her at the index finger. Every time he touched her it felt like a hypnotic caress. The very breath from the sound of his voice made her want to give this condemned relationship a fighting chance. "I love you," she managed to say.

Chapter One
One year later - Birmingham, Alabama

"I don't have to listen to you, you're not my mother."

Cheri stopped dead in her tracks, hearing the nasty tone in which her stepson, PJ, had answered her simple directive. She had been more than tolerant with Preston's son ever since he had come to live with them a little over three months ago. The home she and Preston purchased soon after they married had been her place of serenity; now an eleven-year-old was making it excruciating painful merely to walk through the door.

"I'll put my feet on anything I want to put my feet on," the boy continued. "This is my daddy's house."

Cheri knew that if she did not count to ten and pray there would be hell to pay for both of them. Without turning to face the child she prayed loud enough for him not to miss one single word. "Lord, you know I've been more than patient with this boy, now I'm asking you to please have him out of sight when I turn in his direction. 'Cause Lord, if he's still standing there when I turn around, I know in the depths of my heart that I won't be responsible for my actions. I know I'm going to do something to make his mother press charges against me for child abuse and his father will have no other alternative but to divorce me because I have crippled his child for life. I'm begging you, Lord, please let him be out of my sight so I won't be put behind bars and he can continue to have full function of all his body parts. I'm asking you right now Father in the name of your son, Jesus. Amen." Cheri took a short pause then turned to find PJ gone.

She needed this like she needed a hole in her head. The kid was nasty no matter how nice she was to him. The simple fact was he hated her because she was the reason his parents were no longer together.

PJ had decided he wanted to live with his father after his mother informed him that she had accepted the marriage proposal of her colleague and friend Dr. Stephen Goldberg, so he and his sister Rachel would have to leave the home he grew up in and move in with his mother and her new husband. The child demonstrated his disapproval of the marriage by not attending the ceremony that took place less than three months ago. This certainly caused an enormous rift between mother and son and intensified the hatred toward Cheri.

"Bill, junk mail, bill, bill, junk mail, junk mail ..." Cheri said to herself as she scanned and sorted the mail she had retrieved from the mailbox. "Junk mail... should be a law against so much junk mail. Bill, bill." She paused, looking intently at the next piece of mail.

It was from Dr. Grant Suber, the specialist she had seen less than two weeks ago. No other mail was more important than this one, since she knew it held the results of her latest physical. She laid the other mail on the counter as she entered the kitchen, and just when she was about to tear the envelope open, the telephone rang. "Hello?"

"I got all fifty messages you left me."

Cheri smiled, instantly recognizing her sister Sandra's voice. "You're exaggerating, it was only ten."

"I only listened to two."

"So tell me what the doctor said," Cheri urged her.

"Well, I did what you asked and sent Mama to one of the best, most expensive physicians in Philly and he confirmed what her primary doctor already told us."

"So it is sarcoidosis." Cheri could hear the sadness in her own voice.

"I'm afraid so. The doctor called it pulmonary sarcoidosis, which in half the cases he's seen it's usually temporary and heals naturally, without any treatment, but in Mom's case he said it's serious. He recommends treating the symptoms to help improve how well the lungs and other organs are working."

Cheri moved to sit in a chair at the kitchen table, momentarily forgetting about her own medical results. She blew out a long heartbroken sigh. "I'm coming home. I want to see her."

"Look, Cheri, I had a long talk with Mama after she got this news. She's adamant, baby girl, she doesn't want to see you."

"Why is she being so stubborn?" she asked, even though she knew how unbending her mother had always been.

"You know Mama. She's always said what she means and means what she says. I even told her it was your idea to get a second opinion and that you paid for it."

"What? I told you not to tell her. I'm surprised she agreed to see this doctor."

Sandra laughed. "Oh, don't trip, I didn't tell her until after she saw the man. I thought it might sway her opinion of you."

"Apparently not. She still thinks I'm the scum of the earth."

"You and I will not get into an argument about this. You know I love you, Cheri, even though you're a home wrecker. Now you know this subject is a sore spot for me and Mama." Their father had left their mother for another woman and Cheri's sister's husband had repeated it three years ago. "So please, let's not get into this. You and I will never see eye to eye on this matter."

Cheri cleared her voice. "How did they say she got this disease? You said it's not cancer, right?"

"No it's not cancer. All the doctors told me the same thing. No one knows exactly what causes it. It could have been from bacteria, or viruses, or chemicals."

"Is it genetically connected?"

"No one knows for sure. We haven't had anyone in our family have this illness that we can account for. But I was told that someone with the right genetic predisposition had a possibility of provoking the immune system to develop the inflammation associated with the disease."

After a long pause Cheri said, sadly, "You'll keep me abreast of how she's doing?"

"You know I will."

"Thanks, Sandra."

"You're welcome."

"By the way, have you been able to ask Mama if anyone in our family has had problems getting pregnant?"

"Oh, yeah, I did. She knew it was you who needed to know."

"I figured she would. I'm the only one who's childless."

Sandra giggled, "That's true. She said never in the history of our family has any woman been unable to bear a child. That is, none that she knows of."

Cheri waited as the phone went silent for her sister to give her mother's entire comment, but her sister didn't say any more than that. "I know that's not all she said."

"No, it isn't. And I'm not going to be so heartless and tell you more. What I said is all you'll hear from my lips."

"I can only imagine, but knowing Mama like I do, she probably said, she's getting exactly what she deserves, or God has shut up her womb or something paraphrasing the Bible, she's reaping what she sowed," Cheri said mimicking her mother's voice.

Sandra laughed heartily. "You're not even close."

Cheri didn't find the conversation funny. "Then her heart is harder than I imagined."

"Well, if there's any consolation, no one in the history of our family has ever had sarcoidosis, either. That is, no one that she knows of." Sandra heard a sniffle after a moment of silence. "I'll call you with any changes," she said and abruptly ended the call.

Cheri and Sandra had a love-hate relationship. Like her mother, Sandra had never approved of Preston. He was a married man, someone Cheri should have deemed untouchable.

"You have to be a real fool to even have that man in your presence after what he did to you," Sandra told her sister at the time, referring to Preston marrying Nadine instead of Cheri.

Cheri picked up the envelope from her doctor and read the results. As she scanned the pages a tear slid from her eye. She refolded the paper, sliding it back into the envelope, and reached for the telephone. She pressed one number activating the speed dialing.

"Hey, it's me."

"Hi, babe, I know I'm a little late, but I'll be home within a half hour," Preston said.

"No, it's okay. I just wanted to ask you to bring something home for you and PJ to eat tonight. I really don't feel like cooking."

"Just the two of us? You've already eaten?"

"No, I'm not very hungry. Besides I had a late lunch."

"Okay, I have some exciting news to share with you when I get there."

"Hint, hint?" she teased.

"No, I'll tell you when I get there."

"Uh-huh." Cheri placed the phone on the base and headed for her bedroom.

She opened the top drawer of her dresser and tossed the letter in. "God what is wrong with me?" she asked aloud in frustration. She had been trying to get pregnant since she and Preston had gotten married over a year ago. She had gone to three different physicians and each of them came to the same conclusion: nothing! There was nothing physically wrong with her that would prevent her from conceiving a child. It was even suggested that her husband be tested. She explained that her husband had fathered children, one being the pregnancy she had terminated without Preston's knowledge when she was only twenty years old. So she knew testing him would be a waste of time and money.

The abortion she had was never discussed with anyone. She had gone to Temple University Hospital alone for the initial consultation, and on the day of the procedure her cousin, Greg, accompanied her, who she lived with at the time in an apartment near the university. As far as she knew, Greg never told a soul about it. Something had to have been damaged during the procedure, so that had to be the reason why she could not conceive now.

Every time Cheri thought about that it brought tears to her eyes. There was so much going on at that time and getting pregnant had been an accident that could only added more fuel to the fire.

She stepped to the mirror in her bathroom, looked at herself and sadly said, "You have truly jacked up your life, girl." She should never have terminated that pregnancy. To this day she was still haunted by it." She blew out a long sigh. She had repented about that same sin so many times she had lost count. She had to get her mind off that time of her life before she lost control. Her hormones were already on edge since that time of the month was approaching.

She disrobed and stepped into the shower not able to take her mind off the letter and connecting it to the past.

"I guess I deserve this," she said to herself. "Childless, that's my verdict," she heaved a sigh as tears involuntarily began to fall from her eyes.

Preston never talked about having more children. The last time she and Preston talked about it, he was still married to his first wife, Nadine. She remembered the argument like it was yesterday.

"I need to get out of this relationship. I want to get married and I want children. Why can't you understand that?"

"I understand. I just can't stomach you being with another man."

"You're with another woman. Every time you leave here you go home to your wife and children. What do I have, Preston?"

"You've got me. And that has to be enough."

"I want babies of my own. Why can't I have just one, one is all I'm asking for."

"Because it's not right and it wouldn't be fair to the child to be born out of wedlock," he answered immediately leaving the apartment in a huff, slamming the door behind him. Why had she not left him then? She had more than enough opportunities to walk away, yet she stayed.

She and Preston had separated once for three months. It had been his way of attempting to live a holy life. It was during that time her childhood friend, Curtis Evans, asked her to marry him. He had promised to give her the life she so desired and all the babies she wanted to have. She had seriously thought about it, but each time her mind said yes, her heart said no. She just could not imagine life without Preston, even if it was stolen time from his wife and children.

Now, she had Preston, yet she was still unhappy.

Adoption may not be a bad idea. Since Preston already had children it just may be the right thing for them. "Lots of children need a loving home," she murmured with the intention of convincing herself.

How had her life ended up like this? When she met Preston during her first year in college he was an unmarried senior. At the time, Cheri did not know Preston was engaged to marry in just a few months time and in the beginning that fact remained hidden from her. After that initial meeting, it wasn't long before Cheri and Preston shared most of their free time together and by the end of that first semester, she knew she was deeply in love with the minister in waiting, Preston Matthew Owens.

He came to meet Cheri's family during winter break her freshmen year in college. At the time her mother, along with the rest of the family, thought him to be a nice young man. Her sister Sandra had called him a good catch, nevertheless Cheri was encouraged to concentrate on her studies and to graduate without incident.

It was months later during spring break that Preston decided to take Cheri to meet his family. It was the day she found out that Nadine Carter was Preston's fiancée and a day she would never forget.

Cheri sat in the living room of his parent's home waiting for them to come into the sitting room to meet her.

"You say your father is a deacon?" She was nervous to say the least.

"No." Now stop fidgeting." Preston admonished.

"I'm fidgeting because I'm uneasy about this. I told you I wasn't ready to meet your people."

"Well you have to be ready. I told them about you and they asked me to bring you home so they could see who I keep bragging about. Besides, they're trying to marry me off to another woman."

"What?" Cheri didn't know if he was joking or telling the truth and she communicated that with the look on her face.

"I should have told you that they want me to marry Nadine Carter. She's a really nice girl, but I'm not in love with her. I'm in love with you. I want to marry you," he said with a direct stare.

He had never spoken of marriage before. Not even in a joke. "You can't be serious," she gazed right back into his brown eyes and he didn't have to say anything, the truth was set within.

No, it couldn't be. She misunderstood what he said. "Why did you wait to tell me this now?" She whispered. He better have a good explanation.

"Cause I didn't know I was going to fall in love with you."

She was stunned into no reply.

"I should have known the first time I saw you that I was in trouble. It wasn't long before I knew I was falling head over hills in love with you. I know now, I can't marry her. I want you."

It had to be real, he said it a second time.

She gasped upon hearing the footsteps of the people who could only be his parents. There was no time to react to his admission.

"Here they come," he said softly.

Both of them stood.

"Preston, sweetheart," his mother pressed her lips to his cheek.

"Hi, Mother," he hugged her firmly. He reached out his hand to his father, "Dad."

"Hello, son," he shook his hand. "And is this the young woman you told your mother and me about?"

"Yes, this is Cheri Anderson. Cheri, this is my father and mother, Bishop Charles Owens Jr. and Mrs. Della Owens"

Bishop, Oh my God, "Pleased to meet you both," rolled from her tongue with her hardly recognizing her own voice. She shook both their hands.

"Come, lets sit and chat a while," Mrs. Owens said as she directed them to sit down.

"So young lady, my son tells me you're a communication's major."

"Yes, Sir, I am." She answered remembering all the manners her mother had taught her.

"What do you plan to do with a major like that?" He asked point blank.

"I'm interested in journalism. Hopefully, I can get a job at a newspaper or maybe even a local news station in the Tri-State area."

"Is that right?" Bishop Owens commented.

Cheri smiled, "yes, Sir."

"She could even teach if she wants to, English lit, public speaking, or something like that," Preston added with a nervous smile.

Mrs. Owens cleared her throat. "Well, dear," she spoke directing her attention to her husband, "this is her first year of college. Most students change majors two or three times before getting their degree."

"That's true," he answered his wife then turned in Cheri's direction. "What do your parents think about your choice to major in communications?"

Cheri thought for a moment and answered them honestly. "My mother said she didn't care if I got a degree in dog catching as long as I got one."

Preston and Cheri both laughed, but found shortly thereafter that his parents did not find the remark humorous at all. They stared at them both.

"Lighten up you two, it was a joke," Preston said trying and failing to ease the moment.

"This is not the time for jokes. You've informed us that you are in love with this woman and that you are seriously thinking about breaking off your engagement to Nadine."

"Dad, I think it's best to end it now before making a mistake I'll regret for the rest of my life. Besides, you all are the ones that think I should marry Nadine. It was your idea," he pointed to his father, "I proposed marriage to her before I felt I was ready."

"What's wrong with Nadine?" His mother asked.

"Nothing's wrong with her, I like Nadine. I'm just not in love with her," Preston answered as he took Cheri's hand in his.

"Oh, there's something wrong with her alright. She hasn't let you dishonor her," his father answered looking at Cheri with disapproval.

"What does that suppose to mean?" Cheri asked not believing her ears.

"Dad, please don't do this," Preston warned.

Cheri stared at Preston's father. "What are you saying, Mr. Owens?"

"I'm saying this relationship shouldn't have started." He turned to his son, "you don't come home anymore on weekends and I heard you've been spending a lot of time with her," he pointed to Cheri.

"Dad, I can't help that I fell in love with her."

"Oh, Preston, love is more than passion," his mother heaved a sigh.

"No, say it like it is, sex, it's more than sex, son. You've been beguiled and this is beneath you."

"What?" Cheri roared, "You think I'm less than you and your family?"

"That's not what he's saying," Preston answered for his father.

"Charles," Preston's mother called to her husband in a warning manner to remain calm.

"Nadine comes from a good family," Bishop Owens barked.

"Charles," Mrs. Owens cautioned more forcefully.

"You think I'm not good enough for your son?" Cheri asked wanting an answer.

"Baby, that's not what he's saying," Preston answered again for his father.

"It can't be, because he doesn't know me. None of you know anything about me."

"I know all I need to know about you," the Bishop answered with an air of pride lacing his words.

"What can you know other than what your son told you?" Cheri watched him turn to his wife with a smirk on his face.

"Mother, Dad, I didn't bring Cheri here to be treated like this. I'm really surprised at both of you."

Mrs. Owens ignored her son and said, "Cheri, I don't judge people on their family history. However, we are a product of our environment."

Cheri nodded, "I think I understand." What else could it be? Preston's parents had gotten information about her background. However, she was not aware of anything so detrimental in her past that it would make her unworthy of Preston. So what, she failed Spanish in her junior year in high school and had to go to summer school. Oh, she just remembered the time she was suspended for being in the locker room with four other girls who were smoking cigarettes. Though she was found not guilty for smoking she was still punished for not being in class. But that could not be the reason his parents found her objectionable without knowing her. Her mother was a devout Christian. Cheri had been raised in a Christian home. They may not have been Baptist, but Methodist teaching wasn't that far off.

"Son, we're just trying to keep you from making the mistake of your life. The grass always looks greener on the other side."

"You see, that's what I'm talking about. You can't run my life. If I want to be with Cheri then I'm going to be with Cheri."

Mrs. Owens directed her attention to Cheri. "I can tell you're a sweet girl. I have no doubt about that. It's just that Preston has really never had an interest in anyone other than Nadine and we naturally thought that his heart was with her.

"Now don't sugarcoat this thing. Her grandmother was a whore and so is her father."

"Dad," Preston could hardly believe his father's outburst.

"You knew my grandmother?" Cheri was astonished.

"Your grandmother, Sarah Anderson, had eight children, two by her husband and six by your grandfather Bernard Coles who she knew was a married man."

"What does that have to do with me?" The question seemed fair.

"Your father was the third son of Sarah and Bernard. He left your mother for the woman he now has two children with. The cycle continues because he has not married the woman he left your mother for either."

Cheri was flabbergasted. She had no idea her father had other children. "How do you know this?" She asked with a shaking voice.

Preston gasped Cheri's elbow for support. "Dad, you know this is wrong. She hasn't seen her father in years."

"Then I'm sorry. I didn't know that. But the facts are still the facts."

Cheri moved on wobbly legs and retrieved her purse from the sofa. She turned to Preston and said, "I'll wait for you in the car." She walked out of the room and out of the house without anyone saying another word in her presence.

It wasn't long before Preston came to the car. Cheri was still stunned. Holding tears at bay she murmured, "I wasn't expecting that."

"I wasn't either," he answered with an edge of regret in his voice.

"How could you come from a man so vile?" Cheri really wanted to know the answer to that question.

"My father has strong beliefs."

"Don't make them right," She glared at him.

He locked eye contact, "I agree. But he's still my father."

Cheri turned away from his gaze. "Yes, you're right. It's obvious that they don't approve of me. I'd hate for you to go against your father for a silly thing like love."

"Don't be overdramatic with me," he said accusingly. "Don't you think I feel bad enough for how this whole thing turned out?"

"You should have been upfront and honest with me, Preston. I found myself under attack and I never saw it coming," she argued.

"You're right. I should have told you about my pending marriage to Nadine, but the fact of the matter is I didn't. And do you know why? I'll tell you why. It's because when I'm with you nothing else matters to me, especially her."

"Then maybe I'm just a way of sowing your oats."

He was surprised she said that. "What?"

"Your father seems to know we've been sleeping together."

"What are you talking about?"

"He said Nadine wouldn't let you defile her. Seems he knows I've been defiled and deflowered by you."

"Look, I've been seeing her since we were freshmen in high school. At one time I really liked her. I thought we would marry, but since I met you I know now I don't love her at all."

"You've been dating her since high school? What is that about seven or eight years?"

Preston dropped his head not giving her a verbal answer.

"Take me home," she ordered.

"Cheri, please, you must understand… I really never dated anyone else. I'd never been interested in anyone until I met you."

"Take me home," she was on the verge of breaking out in tears.

"No, we need to get things straight between us before you…"

"I don't want you to say another word to me, Preston. Just take me home," she ordered between clinched teeth so she would not shout at him.

"Cheri…"

"Now," that time she did shout.

Cheri blinked back tears remembering that time as if it were yesterday. From that day until now she and Preston's father had no communication at all.

ଧ୦ଓ

PJ had turned his music up so loud that the floor was shaking. Cheri closed her bedroom door knowing he spitefully jacked up the volume. She didn't feel like arguing with him. She had too much on her mind.

After showering, she put on silk pajamas and was lying across the bed when Preston came into their room.

"Hey, why didn't you tell PJ to turn that music down?"

"I say as little as I have to where your son is concerned," she answered flatly.

He glared at her, "I could hear the music as soon as I got out of my car which I parked at the curb. How could you stand it?"

Cheri never told Preston that living in the house with his son had turned her once tranquil home into a torture chamber. It was her hope that eventually PJ would be at least civil toward her.

"So, what is your great news?" She asked as she watched him place a bag on the dresser.

"I have a new position and a raise starting next week."

"Wow, that's great! So what is your title now?"

"I'm director of human services."

"That's impressive. Wow! How did this come about?"

"Well, when Simon died, they opened up the position to anyone with a master's degree. I put in an application, and I had an interview last Friday and they told me I had the job just before you called me this afternoon."

"You never told me you applied for it."

"I know. I didn't want to say anything just in case someone else with more seniority got it."

"Well, I'm proud of you." She pressed her body against his and kissed him tenderly.

He looked down at her and placed his hands on her hip. "Don't you want to know how much more money I'm making?"

"Sure." She answered as she began to unbutton his shirt.

"I'll be making twenty thousand more a year."

Cheri smiled, "well, I guess you can't say I make more than you now."

"I feel better knowing we have a little more room in our budget for some fun stuff."

"Well, since your ex-wife has married, it's my understanding that you no longer have to pay her alimony."

"Ah," was his reaction from her touch. "I'm going to eat my food, take a shower and then we're going to finish what you've started here."

Cheri smiled and moved to sit on the side of the bed after hearing a knock on their bedroom door.

"Come in," Preston answered.

PJ pushed the door open. "Dad, I can't eat this sandwich."

"Why not?" He asked after taking a bite of his own.

"It has onions on it."

"Then take the onions off."

"I can still taste them. Besides, I don't like chicken sandwiches."

"Then go in the kitchen and make you a peanut butter and jelly sandwich."

"Why Cheri can't cook?"

She couldn't believe the audacity of this child.

"Because she doesn't feel like cooking tonight, son, so deal with it. Besides, you've been complaining about her cooking since you've been here."

"Well, her food tastes better than this sandwich!"

Cheri shot a look at PJ and asked with as much pleasantry as she could muster, "What do you want me to make for you?"

"Can you make me one of those cheese steaks you made the other night?"

Cheri thought about how the boy had devoured that sandwich enjoying every morsel. Plus she figured this was another opportunity to win him over. The barrier between them was huge and would take a lot of time to break down. "Sure, I can do that."

"Can you make it with a lot of cheese?"

She grinned at him. Could it be that his voice held a little excitement in it? "Extra cheese, you got it."

"Baby, the boy can eat what I gave him or make a sandwich on his own," his father pressed.

"It's no bother, Preston. It'll only take ten minutes to make a Philly cheese steak without onions."

Chapter Two

"Good evening, Pastor Wright. Sister Carmen said you wanted to see me before I left this evening."

"Yes, Brother Owens, please come in. Shut the door and have a seat."

Preston nodded feeling a little uneasy not knowing why he had been summoned to the pastor's office.

Pastor Wright spoke soon as he sat down. "Deacon Taylor told me how well the adult Bible class has been doing since you took over."

"I'm glad he's pleased."

"Well, he has to be pleased since all the members have been raving about your knowledge and understanding of the scriptures."

"Well, preparing has taken up a lot of time so I'm glad tonight was my last night teaching."

"I don't think your students like that fact at all. Speaking of which, since they thought so much of you I decided to slip in the back of your class to see for myself, and I've come to the conclusion that they are right, you're good, Son. I also noticed the class has grown three times in size and best of all, they are enthusiastic about learning."

"I've truly enjoyed the opportunity, Pastor. But I'm so glad that Deacon Cannon has recovered from heart surgery and will be back next week."

Pastor Wright stared at him in wonderment for a few moments. "Are you ever planning to tell me, Son?"

Preston was startled by the inquiry and with bewilderment on his face he wanted to know, "what are you talking about? Tell you what, Pastor?"

The pastor tilted his head to one side with a smile on his face. "That you've been called to the ministry."

Preston gave a nervous chuckle, "I have no intentions of telling you any such thing."

"You may not want to admit it, but it's there none the less. Anyone with an ounce of spiritual awareness can see it, Son. It's in everything you do, everything you say and in how you teach. It's in the very way you carry yourself."

"Sir, I mean no disrespect to you, but I have no intentions of trying to fill shoes as large as yours. My intentions for being here is to help this church in any way possible."

"I'm glad to hear you say that." Pastor Wright stared at Preston suspiciously, tilting his head to the other side and asked, "What's the name of the church you came from?"

"I don't believe I've ever said I came from any church."

"But you came from somewhere. Who's your former pastor?"

Preston blew out a long sigh, "What is it that you want to know about me?"

"Brother Owens, I've watched you teach tonight and your style is captivating. You delivered your lesson as good as any preacher, even though you weren't in the pulpit."

"Oh, so you have a problem with my style? But tonight ends my obligation, so my technique won't be a problem…"

"Now, wait just a minute and let me finish," Pastor Wright adjusted himself in his seat. "You're passionate about the Word of God and it shows. People know when you're real and that's what's drawn them to you."

"I simply plant the seeds. It's the Lord that gives the increase."

"See, see how you talk. You won't even give yourself an ounce of credit. Well, I'm thanking God you're part of my congregation."

Preston smiled knowing deep in his heart he found a lot of joy in teaching the adult's Wednesday night Bible study. It gave him a temporary platform to deliver God's message, and satisfy some of the people's appetites who have a hunger for knowledge.

"When I looked out into the pews tonight I saw people in your class that don't even belong here. Tonight you had more butts in the seats than I have at the eight o'clock service on Sunday mornings."

"Well, everyone knew it was my last night teaching so that's why so many were here. Besides, there's no way I could upstage you for a Sunday morning early service, nor would I want to. People just like to sleep in late on Sundays. They prefer the eleven o'clock service over the eight, that's all."

"Hogwash, there's more to you than meets the eye," Pastor Wright snapped.

Preston was quiet as the pastor leaned back in his chair staring at him.

He and Cheri had come to Beulah Baptist Church after hearing that Pastor Wright had lost half of his congregation to a minister who had come from Baltimore, Maryland starting a church not even a mile away. Preston liked working with troubled churches. When he first became pastor of Greater Mount Hope Baptist Church he had a congregation of thirty-two. When he left nearly two years ago the church had three services on Sunday and over three thousand members.

Pastor Wright folded his hands in from of him. "I asked you to see me because I won't be here on Sunday and I need you to deliver the message."

Preston was not sure he heard the man clearly. "Uh, Pastor, you are joking, right?"

Pastor Wright leaned back in his chair. "No, this isn't a joke."

"Pastor, when I said I'd help you any way I could, that excluded your pulpit. I'm simply a teacher."

"Then teach them a good lesson on Sunday morning. Deacon Taylor seems to think you can handle it and so do I."

Preston did not know what to say. When he was a pastor there was never a time he would have considered putting an unknown in his pulpit. "Pastor, you need someone who is qualified to stand in your place on Sunday morning."

"Yes, yes so I've been told, and when I did find someone who was qualified, my congregation was confused for two weeks. Did you know I had to get in the pulpit to clear up the nonsense that man told from my platform?"

"No, I had no idea," Preston answered truthfully before casually asking, "Which service do you want me to… to teach?"

"The eight and eleven o'clock services," he responded.

"Both services," the comment came out like a question, because Preston was in total amazement. "I don't think that's a good idea, Pastor."

"Yes, both, and why isn't it a good idea?"

"People don't want a Bible study on Sunday mornings. They get that during the mid week."

"All the people don't attend Bible study, you know that. Besides, some folks need a good teaching to instead of preaching at." Pastor Wright turned the page of his date book and began to write. "You'll do just fine, you'll see."

"Pastor, I'm sure Minister Grant would welcome the opportunity to minister and since he's been here for…"

Pastor Wright practically slammed his pen on the desk and shot Preston a stunned look. "Who do you think messed my congregation up the last time?" He said with a slightly raised voice.

Preston was flabbergasted, "no."

"Oh, yes. So you see son, I need you more than you know." Then the pastor beamed, "I remembered the day you and your wife walked into this church. The Lord told me then to keep my eye on you. I knew from that first day you were going to be a great asset to this ministry. Son, I know you may not agree with me, but you think you chose Beulah Baptist when it was actually God who sent you to us."

Preston smiled, "Thanks for sharing that with me. You really know how to pump a man up."

Pastor Wright smiled in return. "I've asked you what church you've come from and you've been reluctant to tell me. There's a reason why and one way or the other, it's going to come out."

"If you want me to…"

Pastor Wright held his hand up stopping him abruptly. "What's done in the dark always come to the light. You may want to talk to me before that time. I'll let you be the judge of that. I won't ask you again, so when you're ready, come to me and we'll talk."

Preston did not utter a single word. During a moment of silence the two men stared at each other. Feeling pressured, Preston simply nodded his understanding.

"Good." Pastor Wright stood and reached out his hand for a shake.

Preston gasped it firmly and gave him a half smile.

"It's going to be all right, Son. You'll see. God has a way of working things out, no matter how low or how deep it may be."

"Thanks, I needed to hear that."

Pastor Wright reclaimed his seat. "Now, you have a few days to get ready. You let me know if you need anything between now and Sunday. Bernice," Pastor Wright called to his wife who is also his secretary.

"Yes, Pastor," she was at the door almost instantly.

Pastor Wright smiled, "I know you were eavesdropping."

She grinned with the knowledge that her husband knew her so well. "Not intentionally."

He shook his head, "Give Brother Owens our schedule for the Baptist Convention Conference."

"Certainly," she quickly left the room.

"I want you to talk with your wife and see if the two of you wouldn't mind going along with First Lady and I."

"No, Pastor I couldn't consider going to anything like that right now, I just…"

"You don't have to give me an answer now, but I want you to really think about it. The church will pay all your expenses. So the conference won't cost you one brown penny."

The pastor's wife appeared as quickly as she left. "Here's the itinerary, Brother Owens. Tell your wife that I guarantee the conference will not be boring. We'll even get some shopping in."

Preston smiled, "Shopping… that alone will cost me fifty thousand brown pennies."

The Pastor and his wife both laughed. "Well, those pennies I can't help you with. Honey, please let Brother Warren know I'll see him now."

Preston folded the flyer about the convention and placed it in his inside jacket pocket and started out the door.

"Brother Owens."

Preston turned in the Pastor's direction.

"I'll be praying for you on Sunday."

ଚୈଓଔ

"You're doing what?" Cheri asked with her voice a whole pitch higher than normal.

"I'm going to give the message on Sunday morning."

"Preston, I thought you said you were finished with the ministry. And how did he find out that you were a preacher?"

"He doesn't' know anything. He told me to teach just like I've been doing for the last few weeks. So what's the problem?"

"I knew something like this was going to happen. I could tell from the first day you stood to teach that first class."

Preston made no reply as he sat at the foot of the bed to remove his shoes and socks.

Cheri continued, "a lot of people have been talking about how well you comprehend the scriptures. I guess what's in you simply comes out."

"Well, I'm glad you see it that way. Pastor told me to give you this."

She looked at the folded papers suspiciously. "What is it?"

"It's information about the Baptist Convention that's coming up. He wants us to accompany him and his wife. All expenses paid."

Cheri stared at her husband's back. "Is this one of the conferences you've gone to in the past?"

"No."

"But it's possible we could run into someone you know, right?"

"It's possible we could run into someone we know anywhere we go."

Cheri turned to the window and shut her eyes tightly, "I don't know about this."

"We have time to think about the conference. It's almost two months away." Without looking at his wife he went into the adjoining bathroom.

Just as Cheri heard the shower running the phone rang.

"Hello." She answered on the second ring.

"Hi, Cheri, this is Tiffany."

"Hey Tiff, what's up?"

"I need a huge favor."

"I can't babysit, Tiff." Cheri blurted out.

"No, I don't need a sitter; I need someone to drop her off at daycare at six in the morning."

"You got the one on one interview with the Governor?" She questioned anticipating a positive response.

"Yes, and I have to be there at seven sharp because it's going to be live or it won't happen. The daycare doesn't open until six thirty and it a forty minute drive."

"No problem, Tiff. Just bring her over in the morning and I'll drop her off on my way to the station. Congratulations!"

"Thanks and thank you, Cheri. You're a lifesaver."

She hung up the phone then took a long sigh.

Tiffany was the other female reporter working for the station. Like Cheri she was adjusting to becoming an instant parent. Her best friend passed away only three months ago leaving Tiffany with one hundred percent guardianship over her three year old, bi-racial daughter, Ava. Tiffany who is a beautiful, single, blonde hair, blue eyed career woman, couldn't even comb the child's hair when she first took custody. But, what had been a real challenge at first was now mastered after a few lessons from Cheri. She smiled thinking about how panicked the woman had been when she first got the child, but after some rearrangement in her daily routine, Tiffany was becoming more than efficient at parenting.

Cheri opened the folded pages Preston had given her about the Baptist Convention and read the schedule of events. Nothing interested her and she had no desire to attend.

Cheri had already taken as much flack as she was willing to from the church community. She had been called everything from a home wreaker to an adulteress and she refused to subject herself to anymore insults. If she went to the Baptist Convention she would only be setting herself up for more verbal abuse from those Bible toting hypocrites who liked pointing fingers at her.

Here in Birmingham, Alabama she had relief from all the criticism, but if Preston had not insisted on them joining Beulah Baptist together, she would be enjoying the Sunday morning service programs that came on television. She had concluded that she could get all the religion she needed by sitting on her sofa. There was preaching on at least one cable channel seven days a week. Plus, she could read her own Bible. She held a degree in communications and she wasn't too bad at comprehending the Word for herself.

However, that was the least of her problems. She needed to talk to Preston about adopting a child. At her age conceiving was more than likely out of the question. She had been trying for over a year to become pregnant and nothing. Her co-worker, Amy, had adopted twins just six months ago after she and her husband tried for over five years to have a child of their own.

"It didn't take us long to get approved for a child," she had told Cheri earlier today. "Getting the child was another story. But I can't complain. We only waited three and half years."

"Three and half years, that's a long time," Cheri grumbled. "But I know they were worth the wait."

"Yes, they were. We wanted a newborn and the parents who gave them up didn't want them separated and not many people wanted two babies at the same time. So when they asked if we would take twins we jumped at the chance."

"Well, I hope I don't have to wait so long. I want to be able to keep up with a small child; I'm not as young as you are."

Amy shook her head. "You are not that old."

"Girl don't let the brown hair fool you and haven't you heard black don't crack?"

Amy laughed loudly. "Yes, I've heard that. Cheri you said that the doctors you've seen can't find anything wrong with you?"

"Nothing, they don't know why I can't conceive."

"Has your husband been tested?"

"There's nothing wrong with Preston. He's conceived two children," she revealed honestly. "I thought I told you that."

Amy nodded her head. "Yes, you did. But the question is, are they really his children?"

Now it was Cheri's turn to laugh out loud. "Girl, his son lives with us. He looks just like Preston. The boy even walks like Preston. His hands and feet look just like Preston's. Believe me I don't need a DNA test to know what my eyes have already confirmed."

"Okay, I'm with you," Amy laughed too.

"That's why I told the doctors to forget testing him. He can get me pregnant and to be completely honest with you he did get me pregnant some years ago before we were married."

"Oh, I didn't know that?"

"Well, it's a time in my life that I'm not so proud of."

"You had an abortion?" Amy surprised herself that she had asked so boldly. The question was laced with curiosity.

Cheri nodded her head. "Could be another reason why I can't conceive now," she mumbled.

"If the doctor saw scarring he would have told you so."

"Hey, what's up with you," Preston asked bringing Cheri out of her thoughts. She reached out her hand to give him the brochure she had on adoption. He looked at the front and flipped it over to the back. "And...?"

"I'm going to read the information you gave me on the conference and I want you to read that."

Preston read the cover again. Cheri noticed almost a hint of confusion on his face. He looked at her. "Are you serious?" he asked disbelievingly.

"Preston, I know you may not want any more children. But you know I've always wanted a child of my own."

"This won't be a child of your own. It'll be a child from someone else and you and I will be responsible for raising it."

"I'm too old now to…."

"Besides, we have PJ treat him like a child you've adopted. Give him some of that love you so badly want to give a child." Preston flung the pamphlet onto the dresser.

"PJ is almost grown, Preston. And the boy hates me."

"He doesn't hate you. Besides, that still doesn't give you the right to tell him he needs to go back home to his mother. You need to be compassionate with him, Cheri. I really expected more from you."

"What?" She couldn't believe her ears. "He told you I said that?"

"He tells me everything. He told me you threatened him bodily harm when he had his feet on the table a few days ago."

"What?" She was in awe.

"A simple get your feet off the furniture would have sufficed. You could have even said your feet belong on the floor not on the table, PJ."

"That's not the way it happened," she protested.

"Oh no, then please enlighten me."

"Forget it. I'm not going to argue with you about your son. Believe him." Cheri picked up a pillow from the bed and moved toward the door.

"Where are you going?"

"I'll sleep in the other room. I need space to think."

"If that's going to adjust your attitude go for it," he said sarcastically.

Cheri stared at him as he answered the phone. "Hello… Hi, Mother. How are you and how is Dad?"

Cheri left the room slamming the door between them. That was another thing that bothered her. He talked to his mother no less than once a week even though he and his father were not speaking. It was his mother that kept him abreast of everything going on with other members of his family. His Aunt Karen had come to visit a few days soon after they moved into this house and his Godmother Denise came here to Birmingham two or three times a year visiting from Wilmington, North Carolina. She knew it was wrong, but she felt envious of these relationships, especially since they kept such secrecy between themselves to dispel any conflict with Preston's father for talking to him regularly and visiting whenever possible.

Cheri had not spoken to her mother in over a year, and she couldn't remember the last time she'd even seen her father, Jeffery Anderson. He had left the family when she was a young: one day he was there … and the next he was gone.

It was Preston's father—the first time she met him—who'd confirmed that Cheri's father had moved on with his life with another woman. It had been both a sting to her pride and a revelation. She remembered calling her mother the following day, perplexed about the whole incident and repeating what Bishop Owens had revealed to her about her father. Her mother had been clear: "he wasn't your father, you only came from him, and there's a difference. And if Bishop Owens is that narrow-minded, then he isn't the man I'd thought him to be!"

Cheri had no idea what happened, how it happened, or why her parents had separated. But now she had every intention of finding out.

Chapter Three

For the next two days, Cheri and Preston barely spoke two words to each other. He called her and told her not to cook because he was taking them out; she declined, so he and PJ went without her. It was Saturday morning and Cheri always made homemade waffles. PJ was the first to join her in the kitchen.

"Good morning!" Cheri greeted him with a plate in her hand, prepared just the way he liked it with strawberries and whipped cream. She set the plate on the table and the sight put a huge smile on the boy's face. "Enjoy," she said, setting hot maple syrup near his plate.

"Dad told me to tell you he'll eat when he gets back. He went to play golf."

Cheri nodded. "Thank you."

Before long Cheri was near the end of her Saturday morning routine of house cleaning. Every room was spotless—except PJ's. "You're not cleaning my room?" he asked, standing in the doorway of Cheri's bedroom.

"No, you're old enough to clean your own room."

"Well, I never had to clean my own room when my dad lived with my mom."

Cheri smiled. "Well, you were younger then. Now that you're older, you can clean your own room. It's not that hard to do."

"Then why can't you do it?"

"Your father was the one who told me to let you do it, so talk to him about it." She knew that would end the conversation. Cheri turned away from PJ to gather the rest of the dirty laundry, stuffing it in a bag. When she completed that task she was surprised to see him still standing at her door. "You need something from me?"

"No, but I'd like to know why you want to adopt a baby."

The question didn't surprise her; she figured Preston might have mentioned it to him. "I was thinking about it. Your father and I haven't really discussed it yet." The truth of the matter was that they were not talking at all.

"Is it because you can't have one of your own?"

Cheri stopped moving. "I'd really rather not discuss this with you, sweetie, so just go on and clean your room."

"I'm not your sweetie and I'll clean my room when I get good and ready," he snarled.

Cheri decided not to even look at the child. The less she saw of him at that very moment, the better off she felt she would be. "I think it's best for you to get away from my door."

"My mom said me and Rachel will be the only kids my dad will have."

If Cheri had been a woman without a heart, she would let PJ have it right now, but instead she remained cool. She had to remind herself that she was the adult and he was simply a child who had been hurt by adult actions. She inhaled a deep calming breath.

PJ wasn't finished. "She told me that she and Stephen were having a baby and it was due in August. She said children are a blessing. So since you don't have any children, I guess that means you've never been blessed?"

She blew out the air that should have calmed her. There was no way Cheri was going to deal with this child another day. She had already gotten vacation approval from her supervisor and checked the airlines for a ticket to Philadelphia; she hadn't had a vacation since she started working for Fox6 as an investigative reporter almost eighteen months ago. She truly needed a break. She had had it up to her ears with PJ's disrespectfulness and his outspokenness. She had to get away before she ended up being a news report, instead of simply reporting it.

Now she felt the familiar pain twisting her stomach and turned to face her stepson. "Why do you talk to me so ugly?"

"Because I don't like you, that's why."

"Is that why you lied to your father about the other night? Because you know I asked you nicely to move your shoes from the furniture. And what was your reply to me? It's my dad's house and I can do what I want to do, yet you told your father an outright lie. And you lied simply because you hate me?" Her voice was shaky.

"My mom said he'll always be my dad. He can't divorce me. Besides, I can tell him anything and he'll believe me over a scant like you."

Ouch, now that hurt! "I've not been anything other than kind to you. Why would you lie to your father about what I say to you? You know I never said anything about you going back home. And you continue to provoke me!"

"Why don't you just leave? 'Cause I don't like looking at you. I don't even like talking to you. You make me sick and I hate you!" There, he'd said it. Even though she knew he hated her, hearing it still hurt nonetheless. "My mom and dad were doing fine before you messed everything up," he continued.

That made her remember why he detested her so much.

"One of these days my dad is going to see just what scum you are."

Cheri took a deep breath to steady herself. "PJ, I didn't ruin the relationship between your parents."

"Yes you did! Just because you're on television and people see that pretty face and you be talkin' all nice and stuff don't mean you are. I know what you did and the people don't. You hurt my mom!"

Cheri wanted to cry. She knew at that very moment in the depth of her heart the child had won. There would be no family therapy. She and Preston would be separating, then divorcing as quickly as possible. She had had enough.

"Okay," she said in surrender. "I'm leaving. And I promise you, I'm going to do my best not to communicate with you while I'm preparing to get out of here since you hate me so much. You and your father can have this. I'm not fighting with you anymore."

Then turning for the first time since she and PJ started this conversation, she found Preston standing in the doorway, pressing his son against the door by his collar, with fire in his eyes.

Her eyes widened in alarm and she shouted, "Let him go!" When Preston didn't obey, she rushed over and demanded, "I said, let him go before you hurt him, Preston."

It took another moment before PJ slid to the floor, holding his neck.

"I'm going to whip your behind!" Preston's voice was laced with disgust.

"Go to your room, PJ," Cheri ordered.

"Yeah, go, and I'll deal with you later," Preston barked.

PJ scurried to his room, slamming his door shut. "I know he didn't just slam that door," Preston said and started to go after him.

Cheri grabbed him by the arm. "Leave him alone."

"What? I'm going to give that boy an old-fashioned beating."

"No, you're not," she snapped.

"He needs a strap on his behind, and I'll tell you, I must be crazy for not being all over him right now," he responded and started out the door.

Cheri grabbed him by the tail of his shirt. "You're going to calm down and talk to him later."

"I'm calm enough," he snapped at her.

"No, you're not. You're upset and I'm not letting you touch him."

He looked at her in disbelief. "Why didn't you defend yourself when I asked you about what happened the other night?"

"You didn't ask me, Preston. You told me what you thought I said and did. Anyhow, I didn't think I should have to defend myself.

"But he lied!"

She nodded. "Yes, he did, and you believed him— just like he said you would."

Cheri could tell he was trying to calm himself as he ran his fingers through his hair to the back of his head. "I'm sorry," he said finally, shame in his voice. "I didn't know he could be so hateful. But now he's got a real problem with me."

Cheri shook her head. "No, Preston, you have to understand... to him, I'm guilty of breaking up his family. And I certainly don't want to be guilty of harming the relationship between the two of you as well. So be careful how you handle this, please."

"I'm sorry. I shouldn't have come off on you the way I did. I didn't know he felt that way about you."

"I've known it from day one. You were so happy about him being here that you never noticed how obnoxious he's been to me," Cheri said flatly.

"You're right. But I'm going to see to it that he gives you the respect you deserve."

"No, I don't want that, Preston. The problem between PJ and me has to be worked out between us. You'll only make matters worse."

He gestured helplessly. "How do you figure that? I stood here and heard with my own ears as the boy spoke to you as if you were a stranger on the street."

Cheri began wrapping the cord around the vacuum. "You have to understand … to him, I am a stranger on the street. He has a beef with me, not you. I'm the one who broke up his happy home. I'm the villain here."

"He can't get away with this."

"We should have been honest with everyone, Preston. Your parents, my mother, and your son should know the truth about this whole thing."

"I did what I thought was right." His voice was stubborn.

"But that doesn't make it right. Your thinking so doesn't make it so." Cheri moved to the closet and put the vacuum inside.

"What's done is done," he said with finality.

"Look, I'm the real victim here," she said, feeling herself losing patience. She sat down on the edge of the bed. "I'm the one who's isolated from my family, and on top of that, your family hates me. It's not just your son, it's everybody in your family." She sighed. "Preston, you're a preacher and you know better than anyone that it's the truth that can make us free. I'm tired. I'm tired of hiding and worrying that someone will find us out."

Preston pulled the door shut behind him and secured it. "What do you want, Cheri? What is it you want me to do now?"

She couldn't believe he was angry; if anyone had the right to be angry, it was her. "Look, Preston, it was your ex-wife that had a baby by another man while you were married to her—and I wasn't even in the picture when that happened! I wasn't the one who ruined your marriage! And I certainly didn't come looking for you after years of no communication!"

"Lower your voice, my son is across the hall."

"And he thinks just like everyone else does, that I'm the bad guy. I'm the one who shattered your happy home. I'm the devil—and the church that you love thinks you're a hypocrite who walked all over his poor defenseless wife."

Preston felt himself cooling down. What could he say? She was absolutely right. He moved toward her. "Baby," he said and tried to take her in his arms to comfort her.

"Don't touch me," Cheri said, standing up and moving away from him.

"Baby," he said again, pleadingly.

"No, I mean it, Preston. Don't touch me. I've come to the conclusion that you care about her more than you care about me. You protect her by not telling the truth and you make me look like the heavy. Nadine's career is intact. But did you think about me, or about my career? I left a job anchoring the morning and noon news on a major affiliate station just to be with you. Did you think about my career and what impact this would have on me? No!"

"Keeping Rachel's paternity a secret wasn't for Nadine's sake, it was for Rachel's sake. She's just a child, Cheri."

"She has a father, Preston! He loves her! Nadine is now married to him! He'll never let her visit you … hell, she barely speaks to you on the phone anymore."

"What are you saying, Cheri?" he asked in frustration.

"I'm saying we need to be open and honest with your son about everything."

He shook his head stubbornly. "My parents never discussed anything with me. They said what I would do, and I did just that. There was no discussion and they certainly weren't open and honest with me."

Cheri felt some triumph. "Yeah, and look where that got you! Married to a woman you told me you didn't love, and now you're living in exile because you can't be open and honest—not even with yourself!" She watched his expression change and knew what she said had hit home.

She was right again. If anything, he should have been honest with their parents. His mother would understand even if his father did not.

Preston paused, remembering the past. After he and Nadine married, Cheri had moved to New York, severing all ties with him. It was years before he saw her again, and then it was in living color on his television screen when she was anchoring the early-morning news. She was even more beautiful than he remembered. Her hair swooped over her shoulder and her eyes sparkled like onyx. He had to see her.

At that time the church was flourishing, but his personal life was in shambles. His wife had been having an affair with a colleague at the hospital where she worked. Preston knew the child she carried could not be his own, since he'd had a vasectomy soon after PJ was born—and he hadn't shared that information with his wife. He waited until after Rachel was born to conduct a DNA test to prove the vasectomy had been performed proficiently. After confronting his wife with the evidence, they decided for the sake of the children to live under the same roof with separate sleeping arrangements.

Cheri's voice interrupted his thoughts. "Look, you need to get ready for tomorrow's message. So I'm going to run you a tub of water so you can soak, relax and meditate."

She moved toward the bathroom.

His focus was back on his son's offensive attitude. "I'm still going to get him."

Cheri stopped in the doorway and said, without turning toward him, "Take your clothes off, Preston, get in the tub and leave that boy alone." Then she turned, making eye contact with him. "It's not his fault he has the wrong impression about me. But you know what, he's right about one thing. You and Nadine would probably still be together if I hadn't come into the picture." She sighed, leaning her shoulder against the doorjamb. "I forced your hand to leave her. If I hadn't allowed you to walk back into my world, you probably would have lived your deceptive life out in misery. Come to think of it, if you'd been honest with me in the first place when we first met, back in college, I'm sure I wouldn't have allowed myself to get involved with you. And maybe I would have married Curtis Evans and had a few children of my own." She stood up again and turned to go. "So leave him alone. He's a victim of circumstance."

Preston shut his eyes tightly. There was a coldness in his stomach. Cheri didn't know the worst of it yet. She wanted children ... and he never told her he'd had a vasectomy.

Chapter Four

Superb! It was the only word to describe the message Preston delivered at the eleven o'clock service.

The eight o'clock service was good, but it was something special about that second sermon that propelled what was good into great, then great into superb. It wasn't just the delivery or the topic. He had an aura that Cheri couldn't describe, something that made the whole presentation a spectacular experience. The congregation was astonished and came to its feet in a standing ovation just as he took his seat.

That second message made Cheri recognize that, without a shadow of a doubt, her husband's place was definitely in the pulpit.

Church folk had, in the past, soured Cheri's perception of religion. Preston tried to make her understand that religion was not about the man-made rituals, but rather about the intimate relationship one had with God. Watching her husband greeting people, she knew that he had a natural ability to balance the two with perfect harmony.

As the congregation began to dissipate, Cheri's eyes drifted to her stepson. He'd been subdued since yesterday's altercation. He sat in the corner of the north exit, watching his father greet parishioners with his head bowed and hands crossed. He had not spoken two words to her since she'd saved him from his father's wrath.

Before she could give it any thought, she went and sat down next to him. PJ was large for his age, but he was still a child. He acted like a child, he thought like a child, and consequently Cheri continued to open her heart to him. She expected him to get up and leave right away, but when he didn't move, she was encouraged to attempt a conversation with him. "You want to go out and get something to eat after we leave here?"

"My dad doesn't want to eat with me," he said and pouted.

She heard the sadness in his voice. "That's not true."

"He said he doesn't want to talk to me." It almost sounded like a question.

"Well, your dad is a little stubborn, and he's not very good at communicating when he's upset. You're a lot like him, you know. Just think how long it takes you to forgive someone when you're upset with them! But eventually you come around—and so will your father."

PJ shook his head. "Yeah, but he's really mad," he said.

Cheri smiled. "He can't be that mad. How could someone that angry preach like he did today?"

When PJ looked at Cheri he returned the smile, catching her off-guard. "Wow, you're handsome when you smile." The smile dissolved almost instantly. The child had to remind himself he did not like her.

She went on. "He preached two great sermons today, and he's feeling pretty good right now. This is a good time for you to act normal and take advantage of this moment," she advised.

"I told you, he's not talking to me," PJ complained.

"So talk to him! Remember, you're his only son. He loves you even when he's annoyed with you." Cheri paused and waited but he had nothing to say.. "Did you enjoy his sermon?"

"I always liked hearing my dad."

Cheri nodded. "I like hearing him, too."

"Can I go with Brandon and Theo to the movies today?"

Hmm, she thought. "That's not up to me. You know you need to ask your father."

They sat in silence until Preston came for them with a wide smile on his face. "You two want to get something to eat with Deacon Shaw and some of the other members?"

PJ shook his head before Cheri could answer.

"Look at me, son," Preston said and PJ raised his head. "What do you want to do?"

He had tears in his eyes. "I want to go home and go to the movies with my friends."

Preston stared at his son a moment. "Pick up your Bible, and get up," he said. He waited until PJ rose from his seat. "Right now I need to know what you want to eat and where you want to eat. So I need you to think about that." He reached in his pocket and retrieved his key ring. "Here, get in the car, I'll be there shortly."

Cheri made a move to follow her stepson and Preston halted her by grasping her hand. They watched him leave the sanctuary. Preston turned to her. "He's been upset since I pinned his narrow behind against that door, and I'm not allowing him to have his way. I spoke to his mother last night and she told me to send him home."

"I'm sure she misses him."

"I told her what was going on, how he's been mistreating you. She said he's had an attitude since she and I separated and it got worse when she told him she was getting married."

Cheri shrugged. "Divorce is hard on a child his age. I know—I was only six years old when my father left my mother. Adjusting to him not being around was really hard on me. The only thing I didn't miss was them arguing day and night."

"Maybe that's why I can't understand him, since I came from a loving two-parent home," he said sadly.

"Look, spring break is coming up next week. That will be a good time for him to go see his mother and sister." Cheri started toward the door. "Let him go to the movies, Preston. He's in the dumps right now and going will give him some release."

"Why are you always on his side? He treats you like trash and you make him a cheese steak. He lied on you and you give him money to go to the movies with his friends. I don't get it."

She continued walking. "I found out that you catch more flies with honey."

PJ had started the motor and was sitting in the backseat with his head down. Preston helped his wife into the passenger side, then took the driver's seat. He looked at his son in the rearview mirror. "If you don't want to eat with some of the members at Golden Coral, where do you want to eat at?"

"I want to go home," his voice was low.

"Look, boy…"

Cheri touched Preston's arm. "Your sermon was excellent, Preston, especially the second one."

"You liked the second one more?"

"Oh, it was off the chain! The first one was good, but I could tell you were holding back. But that second sermon was something that young and old could understand. I could tell you simply let go and let God."

Preston shifted the car into gear and moved to exit the parking lot. "I saw you stand up and clap a few times."

"Any time a sermon makes me stand to my feet, you know it has to be good!" she said.

"Thanks, baby. I was nervous early on. I was trying to teach the message instead of allowing God to just use me. But I relaxed the second time and permitted Him to flow. To be honest, it felt good being in the pulpit again." He smiled as he moved into traffic.

"You belong there, Pastor Owens. Preaching is truly your calling. That was evident today."

As if to emphasize her words, when Preston stopped at the red light, the man in the car next to his blew its horn and hollered, "I really enjoyed that message today, preacher! That was my first time at the church, but I assure you it won't be my last!"

Cheri had chosen a mom-and-pop-style Italian restaurant for their late lunch. All during the meal, she tried her best to mend fences between father and son. But she had an ulterior motive. She needed Preston to be in a positive state of mind when she shared her plans with him.

Once they got home she gave PJ some money to go to the movies with his friends.

Preston allowed it though he was not in agreement; he only did it because he could tell that Cheri wanted the boy out of the house for a few hours. He could only imagine what she had planned to do with the time. And truth be told, he wanted to be alone with his wife. They had been at odds for days and he missed her. She had been so upset with him that she wouldn't let him touch her.

Soon after PJ left, Cheri went into the kitchen and Preston went to their master bedroom to remove his suit. He was in the closet reaching for a hanger and could not find one. He searched her side of the closet, finding plenty. That's when he noticed some of the luggage she kept on the shelf was missing. He pulled open the drawer she keep her under garments in and noticed a large quantity of items missing there too. Then he remembered she had been sleeping in the spare room. So he went there to see if she had transferred some of her belongings there.

In the other room, the bed was neatly made and near the foot of the bed were the missing suitcases. Preston lifted one and noticed it was heavy, no doubt filled with her clothing. He looked around the room and noticed a brown clasp envelope on the dresser. He opened it and found an airline ticket to Philadelphia ... with no return flight.

Cheri made a beautiful tray with chocolate, strawberries, whipped cream, and chilled apple cider. She wanted to make the best of the next few hours. She pushed the door open to their room and found Preston sitting at the foot of the bed. He had only removed his suit jacket and shoes. She would take care of the rest of his clothing herself in just a minute.

"Look what I have for us," she said paying more attention to balancing the tray than she did to him. "I'm going to run a tub of water and we're going to relax in bubbles up to our necks and I'm going to feed you your dessert, my love."

Preston didn't move. Cheri still hadn't noticed that he had her airline ticket in his hand.

After arranging the tray on the dresser she came over to where he was sitting, and she finally realized that something was wrong. Usually he was pleased and excited when she prepared such a tray—it was always followed by lovemaking. Not today. "What's wrong?"

"When were you going to tell me you were going to Jersey?"

Cheri was put off for a moment. "I was going to tell you tonight."

"Well, you're not going," he said flatly.

"Why not?" she asked calmly. She was determined not to argue with him.

He didn't even hesitate. "Because you're not leaving me."

"Preston," she said, "I'm not leaving you, baby."

He met her eyes. "That's what you told my son."

"What?"

"You told him you were leaving."

Then she remembered her conversation with PJ days ago. "I was upset, Preston."

"Well, I'm upset right now and you're not going anywhere." He raised the envelope high in the air.

"What are you doing?"

He ripped it in half and said, "You're not going anywhere, so I hope you can get your money back for the ticket."

It was an e-ticket, so another could be printed. Cheri slid onto her knees in front of him, determined to seduce him no matter what. "You are a trip, but I love you anyway in spite of yourself." She began unbuttoning his shirt.

He was glaring at her. "I'm not playing, Cheri." He put his hand over hers and stopped her. "You need to put your things back in the closet," he said roughly and stood up, moving away from her.

"Preston…" she said softly.

"I'm not playing with you. I see where this is going."

Cheri moved toward him again. Sticking to her plan, she whispered, "I'll deal with the clothes later." She moistened her lips with the tip of her tongue. "Right now, I want you," she murmured as she stroked his face seductively. "I've missed you … I need you." She knew how to break him down and he was never able to resist her charm. She began unbuttoning his shirt again. He felt her warm hand on his chest as another traveled lower and he knew she would get her way. "I want this."

He took a sharp intake of breath. "I'm upset with you." His anger was subsiding, but he had meant what he had said.

She exhaled audibly then communicated all her feelings in a kiss.

❧ℭఔ

Preston was sleeping. After their lovemaking marathon, Cheri should have been exhausted too. But she couldn't relax; her mind was racing a mile a minute.

What happened? She had planned to seduce her husband, to make him so senseless in rapture that he would let her do whatever she wanted and give her anything her heart desired. But the plot had backfired: he'd taken total control. He'd finally extracted from her a promise that she never would say that she was leaving again. He sealed her declaration by whispering in her ear, "You're mine. All mine." He repeated a few times breathlessly, making certain it was clear.

And she had to agree. "Always and forever," she heard herself say.

She never got the chance to explain to him why she needed to take this trip. Because she had no return flight scheduled, he assumed she was going back to New Jersey and leaving him in Birmingham for good.

One of the main reasons for her trip was because she had scheduled an appointment with one of the best fertility doctors in Philadelphia.

She lay on her back watching the ceiling fan spin as she remembered how she and Preston had connected again after so many years apart. She had been anchoring the morning and noon news only a short time when on a Wednesday she opened her apartment door to find Preston Owens standing on the other side of it.

Surprise, then shock immobilized her.

"Hello, Cheri." His voice was deep and sexy.

She forced herself to recover as the shock transformed into the resentment that had built up over the years. Her instincts told her to slam the door in his face. But for some crazy reason she tilted her head to one side and boldly stared at him as resentment turned into annoyance. She wanted him to know she was doing just fine after his attempt to destroy her by marrying another woman.

Preston gave her a half smile after seeing a more mature and beautiful woman than he had remembered. He was astonished because she was even lovelier in person than she was on television. Simply breathtaking. "I've been sending you flowers and candy, and you've never acknowledged any of them. Didn't you receive any of it?"

"I received them and the kids at Children's Hospital are truly appreciative of the stuffed animals you've been sending them as well."

He smiled. "Since you've been sharing my gifts to you with others I know that my coming here today can't be a total surprise to you," he replied.

"You only sent them to my place of work. I had no idea you knew where I lived," she said, not moving from the doorway, not encouraging him in any way.

"It took me a while but I finally found you. You should know the people that work with you are extremely protective!"

Cheri narrowed her eyes. "What are you doing here, Preston? What do you want with me?"

"I need to talk with you."

She almost laughed. "No, that's where you're wrong. You should have talked with me seven years ago. Certainly there is no need now."

"I tried to talk to you. You wouldn't accept my calls," he protested.

"That means I had no desire to communicate with you then, and I assure you I haven't changed my mind."

"Please, Cheri, give me a few minutes of your time."

Cheri looked at him from eyes to shoes then eyes again. "Have a nice life, Preston." Then she attempted to shut the door, but he stopped it with his hand.

"Cheri, please," he begged.

If looks could kill, he would have fallen dead at her feet. "Get. The. Hell. Away. From. My. Door," she said through clenched teeth.

"Just a few minutes, please." He clasped his hands together pleadingly.

Cheri had never seen this side of Preston, this vulnerable side. She remembered a time when she had begged him to walk away from his parents' wishes and follow his heart, just as the old church mother had advised him. She told him they could elope and deal with the aftermath later. But he had lied, telling her on a Friday that he would see her on Monday, knowing all the time he would marry Nadine Carter on Saturday. "I don't want to see your face. I don't want to talk to you. You almost destroyed me, and I despise you for it."

She was still furious with him and had held on to the animosity for over seven years. She was incensed that he had the audacity to show his smooth-shaven, sweet-smelling, cologne-patted face to her front door.

With a voice filled with regret he said, "Well, I succeeded in wrecking my own life." His voice was soft, silky-smooth. "We need to fix this, Cheri. Just allow me a few minutes."

Before she could protest, he caressed her cheek with the back of his hand.

Her intake of breath gave him the hope he needed to continue his attempt to tear down the wall of uncertainty and fear. "I swear I miss you so much. I messed up, Cheri. I know I messed up."

Everything within her told her to step back and put the door between her and that smooth-talking weasel, but she couldn't move.

"I just need to fix this," he continued. "I haven't been living. I've only existed without you. Please let me in so we can talk."

She was mesmerized by his eyes, by the sound of his voice, by the smell of his cologne. Did she really want to hear what he had to say after all these years?

"No," she said and shook her head. "You have a wife. Go home to her and leave me alone." Her voice was shaky, but she meant what she said. She attempted to close the door again, but couldn't: his foot was blocking the door. "Move, Preston," she demanded.

"Five minutes. That's all I'm asking."

"I gave you five years, I think that was enough. Now move." Her temper was about to explode on him.

"I've been a fool, Cheri," he said and his voice cracked. "There's no excuse for my behavior, but as God as my witness, I have always loved you. I just couldn't stand up to my family at the time. But you've been in my heart and on my mind every day ... every single day."

Cheri stared at him. His words mirrored what she had been going through since the day she found out he had married the other woman. All of a sudden she felt like she was beginning to hyperventilate.

"I never stopped loving you, never."

She shook her head. "Liar." Was she having a panic attack?

"Yes, I lied. I lied to myself thinking I could live the rest of my life without you. Thinking time would diminish my feelings for you. Thinking I needed my parents' approval in everything I do. But I can't do it anymore. I don't want to try anymore."

"No." How could she determine his sincerity? Now she was visibly shaking. "Why are you doing this to me? Do I look like Boo-Boo the Fool to you? Or do you think I'm some kind of slut with no morals?"

He stared at her and she stepped away from him, giving him the space to advance further into her apartment. "You know better than that." Immediately she realized that was a mistake. She had to get control of herself and this situation right now before seven years of building her life without him went down the drain.

The first few months after his betrayal, she'd cried every day. Then it took a year to stop dreaming about him every night, and after three years of mourning his loss, she only thought of him occasionally. Then after seven years, just when she thought she was totally free from him, arrived the first of many deliveries bearing his inscription.

"Seeing you on television made me confront my feelings for you. I loved you then and I still love you now. Congratulations and welcome back home.

"Preston."

She has been just fine without him. She proudly raised her head. "No," she said with emphasis.

"I've never wanted anybody but you," he said and pressed even closer toward her, lifting his hand to move a curl from her eye. Before she knew what was happening, she was in his arms and he was kissing her lips.

Cheri was so stunned she never got a chance to put up a fight. Maybe deep down inside she didn't want to.

"I'm so, so sorry. I never meant to hurt you," he whispered.

How could she? No, how dare she allow him to take advantage of her this way? Doesn't he know how much his deceit had incapacitated her? With little effort she attempted to free herself. "I don't want you here," she said, but her words were weak, shallow, and painful.

"I know, and I shouldn't be here, but I am," he said, still kissing her face, her hair, her ears, her lips, until the fight was totally out of her. All the years of emptiness vanished when he deepened the kiss. And when it ended, he held her close, declaring, "I need you. I love you, and I want you."

He unzipped his jacket just before he lifted her from the floor, moving them into the living room. That gave her just enough time to regain her sanity. "Enough." She backed away from him. "And don't come near me, I mean it, Preston."

"Let me..."

"No, you are a married man. I can't be with you this way. You're a minister. How can you even think to do anything against the pulpit?"

Cheri saw him drop his shoulders. "I'm sorry, you're right."

"I want you to leave." She headed to the door and opened it.

"Can we be friends? I promise to keep my hands to myself."

"Not a good idea."

"I won't touch you. I just want to be able to talk to you."

"Why do you want to talk to me, so you can convince me to whore around with you?"

A knock at the door brought Cheri back to the present.

She looked over at Preston; he hadn't moved from his slumber. Cheri knew it was PJ letting them know he was home from the theater, so she got up to open the bedroom door.

"Hey, how was the movie?"

"It was okay," he mumbled.

"Well, okay, goodnight."

He went straight to his room without a reply.

As she closed the door, she wondered how long she would have to endure his attitude. She really did not need the added stress, so she prayed every day for a happy medium.

Instead of going back to bed she went into the bathroom for a long soak in the tub. When she came out Preston was propped up on an elbow looking directly at her. "Where are you going?" he asked, watching as she tied the belt to her robe around her waist.

"I thought I'd watch television for a while. Want to join me?"

"Come here, baby." Preston patted the mattress.

"You aren't still mad at me, are you?" she asked not moving to the bed.

"Didn't we just make love?"

"What's that have to do with my question?"

He smiled; she was right. Some of their best lovemaking had been while they were quarreling about something. "No, I'm not upset with you."

"Then can we talk now?" She really wanted to settle the matter.

"You're not going to Jersey, so there's nothing to talk about."

She sighed. "Preston, after all we've been through, why would you think I'd leave you now?"

"Because I heard you with my own ears tell PJ you were leaving."

"Then you also know I was hurt and angry," she retorted.

"You were serious when you said you were leaving. Don't deny it."

"I just didn't want to fight with your son anymore. As a matter of fact, I'm tired of walking around here trying my best to be overly nice to him when he hates my guts."

"Well, he's going back to live with his mother. She's sending for him during spring break and he's not coming back."

Cheri shook her head. "I don't want you to do that because of me. He'll only hate me even more."

"Is that even possible?"

"Doesn't seem so," she answered sadly.

"Then don't worry about it. He's out of here," he stated with finality.

Deep down, Cheri hated that it had come to this. She wanted PJ to be with his father, but she didn't want to be uncomfortable in her own home either. Yet she felt sad for the boy.

Preston could tell his decision to send his son back to his mother did not sit well with his wife. "Hey."

She looked over at him.

"Don't worry about PJ. He'll be fine."

She nodded then took her bottom lip into her mouth.

"Let's talk about something else," he said. "I've noticed something about you that's bothering me."

What was it now? "What?"

"Your weight. You're getting too small. We were in a restaurant where the food is wonderful and you hardly ate enough for a small child."

"I gained thirty pounds. I have to be careful."

"Where are these thirty pounds?"

"Everywhere," she laughed. "And it doesn't look good when I'm filming my reports."

"You look fine to me, so start eating, okay?"

After a moment of silence she nodded her agreement. "Preston, I want to see my mother. She's ill and I need to try and restore our relationship."

"She won't talk to you, baby, you know that."

"But I want to try. You're able to talk to your mother so you don't understand."

"I do understand," he said. "My father is just like your mother, hateful and mean as hell."

Cheri sighed. "I miss my family. I miss then terribly and I want a chance to get together and see if we can work out our differences. I need you to understand and not be angry with me. Besides, I want to try and get in touch with my father too."

"Your father?" He was surprised. She'd never talked about contacting him before.

"Yes ... I'm older now, and I'm sure he's getting to the age where he may be receptive to me. I want to at the least try and have some kind of relationship with him. We were close when I was a child and I need some answers my mother never supplied."

Preston was silent for a moment. "Why didn't you get a return ticket?"

"I have a return ticket, it's just open. I did that just in case it gets crazy and I need to leave sooner than later, that's all."

Preston patted the mattress again. "Come here, baby."

Cheri went to him and he pulled her into the bed with him. Laying her head on his chest she could hear the beat of his heart. "How long do you plan to stay?"

"One week."

"One week and then you come back home and we'll plan to spend a week together someplace, just you and me, all right?"

She lifted her head to look into his eyes. "You're saying I can go?" She wanted confirmation.

He heaved a sigh. "Yeah, you can go."

"Thank you, baby!" She straddled his body then kissed his jaw several times before passionately kissing his lips.

When their lips parted he whispered, "I know you don't want another round." He was stroking her back.

"What's the matter, you can't take it?" she asked dreamily.

"I'm tired, I did all the work."

"Yeah, I know, and you were wonderful." She smiled at him wickedly. "But it's my turn now." She reached over and switched off the light.

Chapter Five

The airport was crowded. Cheri pulled her luggage behind her, searching for her sister. When she didn't see anyone, she paused near a row of seats, retrieved her cell phone, and dialed Sandra's number. The call went straight to voice mail. Sandra had promised to pick her up, so she had to be here or on her way. The phone rang again almost immediately. "Hello," Cheri answered on the first ring. "Where are you?" She spoke loudly to be heard over the noise airport chatter.

"I'm at home, baby." It was Preston. "I've been trying to reach you over an hour now."

"I had my phone off while we were in the air. The plane landed a half hour ago and Sandra isn't here."

"She's not coming, baby."

"What?" Her stomach clenched in anxiety.

"She's not coming. That's why I was trying to reach you. But don't worry, I contacted Darrell and he's sending his wife."

"Who?"

"Rev. Dr. Darrell Parker Jr., the man who performed our wedding ceremony. He's sending his wife, Jade, to get you."

And there was Jade herself, waving to get Cheri's attention as she approached her. "She just found me."

Jade was out of breath. "Hey, I was at the wrong gate. This is a huge place." She embraced Cheri in a tight hug. "I didn't mean to leave you waiting so—"

She stopped short, noticing the phone to Cheri's ear. "Oops, sorry!"

She smiled at Jade. "Preston let me call you when I get out of here. I can hardly hear you."

"What?"

"I'll call you back!" she shouted and disconnected.

"I was at the wrong gate," Jade repeated.

"Don't worry about it." Cheri was grateful she'd come for her on such short notice.

"Do you have all your bags?" Jade asked.

"Yes. I'm so sorry about this, my sister stood me up and I'm really going to let her have it."

Jade smiled sympathetically. "Well, I'm sure if she could have been here, she would have."

Cheri sighed. "I suppose so," she said. "I just hope my mother is all right."

Jade began leading the way out of the airport. "Oh, dear, Preston didn't get a chance to tell you, did he?"

"Tell me what?"

"Your sister called him. Must have been right after your flight took off. Apparently she's having some financial problems, and she's moved in with your mom." She paused. "I gather that means you can't stay with her."

And she waited until the plane was in the air to say so? Cheri was distressed. "Oh, she should have told me that before I made plans to come here! I need to get in touch with my cousin Greg, maybe I can stay with him."

"You don't have to do that. You're going to stay with me and Darrell!" Jade laughed. "I know Greg wouldn't mind, but his girlfriend lives with him in a one-bedroom apartment so it's probably best you stay with us." She caught sight of Cheri's face and hurried to reassure her. "Look, it's really no big deal. We just moved over the weekend and the house is in disarray, but we have plenty of space. The bedrooms are the only rooms in the whole house that aren't a mess! So you're staying with us. Darrell promised Preston we'd take care of you."

"You're so kind," murmured Cheri, still wondering why Sandra hadn't told her the truth. As they approached the car, Jade popped open the trunk with her remote control. "I'd help you put the luggage in, but I've been instructed not to lift anything heavier than my purse."

"Oh, okay."

It wasn't until Jade slipped behind the wheel of the car that Cheri understood why she had made that statement. "You're pregnant?" Her eyes widened in surprise.

"Yeah, three more months and I'll drop this load and I pray it's my last."

Cheri smiled. "How many does this make?"

"Our third. My baby was only ten months old when I found out — oops, here we go again."

"Well, be grateful. They're a gift from God. Do you know how many women would love to be able to give birth who can't?" Cheri was thinking about herself.

"I'm sure there's a few. And believe me I'm very grateful since I have a husband who wants a house full." Jade gave the attendant her parking ticket.

"How much is it?" Cheri asked, reaching for her purse.

"Relax, I got this."

When Jade drove up to her home, Cheri's eyes widened. "This is beautiful."

"Oh, thank you, girl. Darrell found this place. Hardship case, the guy was about to lose it through foreclosure. He and his wife divorced and both their incomes were needed to support it, so..."

"It was a blessing for you."

"For him too, because his credit was saved and he was able to purchase something he could afford on his income alone."

Cheri nodded.

"We ended up paying half the price for this bad boy. That's the only reason we got it. And if I decide I don't want to be with Darrell anymore, he can afford this place without me. We budget our bills on one salary."

"Don't be silly. You and Darrell will be together until death do you part."

"Well, that's the plan, but you never know." Jade was smiling.

Cheri's mind went to Preston. Just last week she had thought about leaving him. But after what happened with his son, she put the idea to rest.

Jade drove into the garage as it automatically opened.

"You should have driven the minivan. You probably would be more comfortable."

"Probably, but I bought this car for my birthday and I don't drive it much. Most times I have the children with me, so on those rare occasions I'm childless, I get to drive this one!" She unlocked the door to enter the house.

Cheri looked around her. Jade had been right: the house was cluttered with boxes. "Looks like you could use some help."

"A few of my friends were supposed to assist me, but we moved a week earlier than expected. Darrell's been working every day, and since I was the only one able to take some time off, I'm settling us in. It's mostly just small stuff now."

"Well, since I'm here, I can help."

Jade shook her head. "No, I'm not putting a guest to work!"

Cheri touched her arm. "Please? If it weren't for you, I'd still be at the airport with no place to stay."

Jade smiled. "No, you would have called your cousin Greg or checked into a hotel. Girl, you know you don't have to work for room and board."

"I know." Cheri walked into the family room. "This is so nice. I like the stone fireplace."

"Thanks." Jade was fumbling with her phone. "Let me call my mother-in-law. I need to pick up my crumb snatcher."

Cheri's cell phone rang and she knew it was Preston. "Hey."

"Are you all right?

"I'm fine. Thanks for calling Darrell, I'm with Jade now."

"Good. But you probably should just come back home."

She shook her head, even though he couldn't see her. "I'm going to stay a few days. I want to try and see my mother."

He laughed. "Okay, I knew you were going to say that. I'll call you later on this evening. Love you, babe."

"Love you more."

After Cheri ended the call with her husband she tried her sister's number again, only to leave yet another message.

ഇൗരു

Preston's son was pouting. Preston stood in PJ's bedroom doorway watching the boy throw his clothing into suitcases. "Make sure you pack everything," said Preston. "I'll have the school transfer your records."

"I don't want to stay with my mom," PJ complained.

"Well, your mother and I talked about it and we think that's best. You've caused enough havoc in this house."

"So you gonna take Cheri over me?"

Preston paused to get his anger under control. "Cheri didn't do this to you, son. You did. Your attitude has been deplorable and you know it. Cheri is my wife and the Bible says cleave to your wife, not your children. Do I make myself clear?"

"Mommy was your wife, and you didn't cleave to her," PJ said with tears in his eyes.

Preston felt the boy's pain, and he strode into the room and took his son in his arms, hugging him. "You don't understand. You're young, and one day when you're older, I promise to tell you why we split up."

"But I want to know now." PJ squirmed out of the hug.

"It's complicated, son." Preston sighed.

"Is it because you met Cheri?"

"Oh, is that why you've been so mean to her? You think she's the reason why your mother and I separated?"

PJ tossed some more undershirts in his suitcase. "Ronnie said that his parents got a divorce because his father got another wife, just like you did."

"Well, Ronnie doesn't know anything about me and your mother, now, does he?"

The boy shook his head.

"Okay," Preston said. "When you're older, I promise that you'll understand. Haven't I always kept my promises to you?"

"No you haven't. You said I could live with you."

"And you did live with me. It's not my fault that you messed things up."

"But I want to stay here with you, Daddy." There was a catch in his voice.

"That's not possible anymore. You've made Cheri very unhappy living here with you. You lied on her and you've been downright nasty."

"So she wants me to leave?"

Preston shook his head emphatically. "No, she didn't ask me to send you back to your mother. I told your mother what you did, and your mother and I decided that it was best for you to live with her."

"But I don't want to live with her!" he whined.

"Well, I'm sorry about that. But I have a responsibility to handle the problem you created here. You can't go around treating people with no regards to their feelings. You hurt Cheri, son. You know you did, because that was your intention, now wasn't it?"

PJ dropped his gaze to the floor.

"You don't have to answer, but this is called reaping what you sowed. Understand?"

"No."

"PJ, son, you do understand you've been extremely hard to live with. I know you do."

"Okay. But what if I promise to be better?"

Preston shook his head. "Your mother and I have already made our decision. No more discussion. Now, be sure to pack everything. Your plane leaves at seven-twenty in the morning." Preston's cell phone rang and he clicked it on. "Hello?"

"Is this Preston Owens?"

"Yes."

"This is Bishop Taylor, how ya doin'?"

Preston turned and walked slowly out of PJ's room. "I'm fine, bishop, and you?"

"Doin' good. Listen, I tried getting in touch with you earlier today. Got a call from a man name Cornel Wright. I assume you know him?"

"Yes, he's the pastor of the church I attend here in Birmingham."

"He said as much. He also said you preached at his church last Sunday. Said you delivered the message too well to be a newcomer. He wanted to know everything about you."

"What did you tell him?" Preston felt his frustration rising.

"The truth," the bishop answered honestly.

Preston took a deep breath. "Maybe I should have asked how much you told him."

"I told him everything. But only because he told me about plans he has for you that's deserving of him knowing the whole truth."

He sighed. "It was bound to come out at some point. I'm glad it was you he talked to and not some other person who didn't have a clue."

"I agree."

"Well, thank you for that. While I have you on the phone, bishop, I know you offered to speak with my wife's mother."

"Uh-huh."

"I declined," Preston said, "because I was assuming that things would work out with time."

There was a pause on the other end of the line. "But it hasn't?"

"No, sir, it has not."

"Hmm," said the bishop. "When was the last time your wife tried to contact her mother?"

"Today, sir. She's in New Jersey right now."

"In that case, I'll get right on it."

Preston smiled with relief. "Thank you."

"You're welcome. Enjoy the rest of your day."

"You do the same."

Preston ended the call and immediately punched in another number. "Pastor Wright, please. Thank you, I'll hold."

When Pastor Wright answered the phone a full minute later he immediately began defending himself. "Minister Owens, I know I told you that I would wait for you to tell me what you needed to in your own time, but things have changed for me. I need to set some things in order here at the church and I needed to know if you were the man I thought you were. And you are!"

"Pastor, what are you talking about?" Preston asked, baffled.

"I need an assistant pastor. I'm up in age as everyone can see and I need to pass the torch to someone—and you're the one, my boy. I prayed and the Lord sent you to me."

Timing is everything, Preston thought. "Pastor, I'm calling you to let you know I'm resigning from the church membership. I'll be handing in my notice as soon as I can get it typed."

"Oh no! You can't do that!" Pastor Wright exclaimed.

"Pastor, I have too many personal problems to hold a leadership position in anyone's church."

"Who doesn't have personal problems? God works through imperfect people every day. I'm proof of that."

Preston wasn't going to be swayed. "I need to handle my own house before I can think about handling God's house. I'm sure you can understand and appreciate what I'm saying."

"That's exactly why I want you, son. You have integrity. Look, I'll tell you what. After the convention we'll talk about it again, by then ..."

Preston cut the pastor off. "I don't think I'll be able to go to the convention with you and your wife."

"Well, why not? The church is taking care of your expenses."

"My wife and I are really having some issues right now and I need to focus on that."

Pastor Wright blew out a long sigh. "You and the misses will be fine. Life comes with traps along the way, but with prayer and supplication you get past them. So don't allow the devil to use them to keep you from your destiny."

"Pastor..."

"I will not accept a resignation from you, Assistant Pastor Owens. I expect you to take the time you need to get your house in order and after that I expect you to be by my side when I make the announcement to the congregation. You've been in exile long enough. This ministry needs you, and I need you. We both know you belong in the ministry. Your teaching and the sermons you delivered here at this church show evidence of your gift. Now tell your wife we're looking forward to sharing a glorious time with the both of you at the convention six weeks from now."

Preston surrendered. "We'll talk again about this after the convention."

"Sounds good. Now, you have a wonderful day. I'll be praying for you and Sister Owens."

"I appreciate that. I need all the prayer I can get."

"Keep the faith, and you'll be just fine."

Chapter Six

Cheri got up early, spending most of the morning the same way she had the day before—helping Jade unpack boxes and organize the house. She rather enjoyed doing it. It freed her mind from thinking about her sister not showing up at the airport and her own inability to conceive. Sandra finally called her back late in the morning saying she was at work, but would call again when she got off to try and arrange a meeting with their mother.

That's what Cheri wanted more than anything: to simply get to talk to her mother and hopefully her father as well. An investigative reporter for a local news station and long-time associate had offered to find her father; and he had done just that. From the looks of the information she received early that morning, her father had never been in hiding. He'd retired from the Philadelphia police department only three months before. It was a job he'd held since he was twenty-two years old. He had begun his employment there soon after he married her mother.

Now standing at his front door poised to knock, she had doubts. Whatever she did she needed to decide now. What did she have to lose? She took a deep breath, blew it out to calm herself, and then knocked. She hoped he didn't slam the door in her face—or worse.

"Hello, I'm…"

The boy's eyes widened. "Cheri Anderson!"

Cheri smiled. "Yes, and you are?"

"Bradford Anderson."

Cheri extended her hand, "Well I'm pleased to meet you, Mr. Anderson."

The boy giggled.

She kept smiling. "Okay, I'm going to take a guess and say I'm looking for your dad."

"My daddy is your brother."

The statement caught Cheri off-guard. "Well, I'm not sure who your father is, but I'm sure we're related in some way."

"Who's there, Brad?" a woman's voice asked just before the door swung open. The women stared at each other for only a moment. "You're Cheri Anderson from the news."

Cheri smiled. "I used to work for them."

"Oh, my goodness, Dad, she's here!" The woman signaled excitedly, waving Cheri inside. "Come in, come right in." She turned and yelled, "Dad!"

"You know who I am, now who are you?" Cheri asked as she followed the woman inside.

"I'm Tonya, have a seat and I'll get Dad for you."

Cheri nodded. "Okay."

"I saw you lots of times on TV." The boy was still giggling.

"Really, how old are you?" Cheri asked.

"Five."

"You're a big guy for five years old! Are you sure you're only five?"

He giggled even more.

"Ma Chérie Amour." Cheri looked up and there stood her father. He had aged gracefully; though he was thinner and slightly gray, he looked amazingly well. He opened his arms and Cheri seemingly floated over to where he stood. "Daddy," she said and embraced him.

He repeated, "Ma Cherie-Amour."

"No one ever called me that but you, Daddy."

He smiled. "That's because you've always been my darling love."

She leaned back to look at him. "I've missed you."

"I've missed everything. You growing up and becoming the beautiful woman you are."

She hugged him again.

He pulled away first and looked over at the woman who had let her in and said, "Cheri, this is LaTonya Anderson. She's my son Bradford's wife, and the mother of little Bradford over there."

LaTonya smiled. "It's nice to finally meet you. Your father told us stories about how you would interview him all the time when you were a child."

Cheri laughed. "Really, Daddy, I'm surprised you remembered that!"

"Of course I remembered. I figured way back then that I was your first news story."

Cheri smiled. "Only after my Barbie dolls."

"They didn't count, they weren't real."

Little Bradford came to stand next to Cheri. "She's pretty, Grandpa."

"Get over here, boy," his mother scolded him.

"He's fine." Cheri sat down again and motioned for him to sit on her lap. "So why aren't you in school?"

He grinned. "I don't go to school yet!"

"Really?" she asked. "Why not, aren't you five years old?"

He laughed and nodded his head.

"He just turned five last month," his mother answered.

"Oh, so you'll start next term." Cheri touched his nose with the tip of her finger. The boy bobbed his head up and down.

"How's your mother?" Her father asked.

Difficult subject. "She's been ill, but we're getting her the best of care," she answered.

"I'm sorry to hear she's been sick. I hope it's nothing serious."

Cheri wondered what she should tell him about her relationship with her mother. A little at a time, she decided. There was no need to rush.

"Would you like something to drink, Cheri?" LaTonya asked.

"No, thanks." She jiggled Bradford up and down on her knee and he squeaked in delight.

"How's Sandra?" her father asked as he took a chair across from her.

"She's doing fine. She's moved in with Mama."

"Oh, is your mother that ill?" He sounded sincerely concerned.

"No, Sandra moved for financial reasons. She and her husband are separated and have decided to divorce."

"Oh. I'm sorry to hear that."

After a long pause Cheri blurted out, "I've been angry with you."

Her father looked over at his daughter-in-law. "Can you give us some privacy, Tonya?"

"Sure, Dad. Come on, Brad."

"I want to stay." Brad whined.

"Get off your Aunt Cheri's lap now and come with me." LaTonya ordered. Cheri smiled at the comment, feeling a rush of warmth about having more names to place on the family tree.

They were alone when her father rose from his chair and stood by the window. She could tell her comment had made him nervous. "I know you've been upset with me. You have every right to be. I should have fought your mother when she said I couldn't see you and your sister. I had every right to do so. After all, you were my babies, too." He sighed. "But when I was finally able to talk to your sister, she was so nasty and cruel toward me that I figured your mother had poisoned you all against me. I tried to see you a few times after that, and your mother wouldn't allow it. I knew she meant business when I was served with a restraining order to stay away from you all. Plus I didn't want to jeopardize my job. Being a police officer, I couldn't risk being arrested and your mother was angry enough to do that."

His words stung. "Oh, so it's Mama's fault you were an absentee father?"

"No, I should have taken it to court and demanded my rights. So no, it's nobody's fault but my own." He shook his head, taking responsibility.

Cheri wasn't ready to back down. "So how many children did you have with the woman you left Mama for?"

"What you need to know is that I didn't leave your mother; she was the one who kicked me out of the house."

Cheri glared at him. "Of course she did! Because you were having an affair!"

"Yes, I cheated on your mother, but I never had any children with that woman. I tried to explain to your mother that I wanted to be with my family. I tried to apologize for being unfaithful to her but she didn't want to hear it."

Cheri conceded that point. "She's always been stubborn. But you hurt her and the residue from your betrayal lingers to this day."

He sat down across from her, leaning forward. "I'm sorry. I know I was wrong, but I wanted to be forgiven and come home. I didn't care nothing about that woman

I cheated on your mother with. I ain't trying to make no excuses, but I was young when I married your mother and I tried living on both sides of the fence." He took a deep breath. "But I broke off the relationship I had with the other woman 'cause I loved your mother. I tried—and I mean really tried hard—to get my family back. Your mother wouldn't bend. She told me she wanted a divorce and, after a year, I met Sarah and a year later we had Bradford and two years after that Mark came."

"So I have two brothers?"

"You had two brothers." He paused. "Mark died when he was sixteen from sickle cell anemia."

"I'm sorry." What else could she say?

"No," he said and shook his head sorrowfully. "I'm the one who's sorry. I made mistakes that I'm still paying for."

Cheri tried to sound cheerful. "Well, I'm glad to see you moved on with your life. Mama was never interested in dating or getting involved with another man. She wrapped her life around her daughters—and now she's all alone."

"I'm alone now, too."

"You and your wife are separated?"

Her father gave her a puzzled look. "Sarah passed away more than ten years ago, Cheri. And I never married Sarah, because I'm still married to your mother."

"Excuse me?"

"Your mother and I never divorced because I refused to file."

Cheri was amazed at this information. "She never filed?"

"She told me when I was ready to have my attorney send her the paperwork, she'd sign it. I was never ready to file, so we just stayed married."

"She's been married to you all this time?" Cheri marveled at the information.

"Well, not unless she divorced me without me knowing," her father said with a sad smile.

                ഇ౮ൽ

Cheri made it to her doctor's appointment with only ten minutes to complete the new-patient forms. She hated leaving her father's house so abruptly, especially since she was finally getting answers to all the questions she'd had for years. But she couldn't be late for this appointment and risk the doctor not seeing her. Thank goodness she had set Jade's car navigation system, making it easy for her to get there swiftly even with the thickening traffic.

Only a moment after she filled out the necessary paperwork she heard someone greet her. "Hello, Cheri."

"Nadine." Cheri was surprised to see Preston's ex-wife standing over her, and she stood up politely. "How are you?"

Cheri stood staring at her protruding belly. PJ had mentioned that his mother was going to have a baby.

"I'm … I'm good. You're seeing one of the doctors here?"

Cheri hesitated before nodding.

Nadine immediately noticed her elusiveness. "It's none of my business, forgive me for asking. I picked up PJ from the airport this morning. Preston told me how he was treating you. Believe me, we had a long conversation about it and he knows he was wrong."

"He's hurting." Cheri murmured.

"It still doesn't give him the right to be disrespectful and downright mean to you."

Cheri nodded. "He's only reacting to what he knows," she said. "Maybe if he knew the truth, things would be different."

"I'm sure they would be. He'd probably detest me more than he does now."

Cheri shook her head. "Your son loves you," she said, feeling a piercing pain in her heart. Nadine had a son, Preston's son, and she felt ashamed because at that very moment she was jealous of that fact.

"But he despises my decision to leave his father," Nadine rejoined. "And he especially despises me for marrying another man."

Cheri took a risk. "I never understood how or why all this happened in the first place. I mean, you and Preston are intelligent people and…"

Nadine stopped her abruptly. "I think we need to talk, you and I. My office is right around the corner. Do you mind?"

"I don't know if that's a good idea, Nadine. My appointment is in any minute."

"Which doctor?"

"Carter." She answered before thinking about it, and right away Cheri saw the stunned look on Nadine face.

She turned to the receptionist station. "Will you let Dr. Carter know I have Mrs. Owens in my office?"

"Sure, doctor," the young woman behind the desk answered with a smile.

Cheri followed Nadine to her office and after she sat in the visitor's chair she spoke. "I had no idea you worked here."

"Not many people do. I started about two months ago. I specialize in infertility."

Now Cheri understood why she was taken aback when she told her which doctor she was there to see. "Oh."

"You were saying you didn't understand why Preston and I let this happen."

"Look, I'm not judging. It's…" Cheri paused.

"Just ask me what you want to know. I have nothing to hide from you."

"I have no right. I'm wrong for even sitting here in your office." Cheri stood up indecisively.

Nadine sighed. "Look, I never had any animosity toward you. I actually like you."

Cheri remained, standing not moving toward the door. She shut her eyes tightly as Nadine continued.

"What happened between Preston and me came about because we shouldn't have married in the first place. I was in love with Stephen, and he was in love with you."

"He lied to me," Cheri said. "I didn't even know that he had gotten married until I read about it in the newspaper."

Nadine raised her eyebrows in surprise. "I didn't know that."

"He tried to contact me afterwards, and I wouldn't see him or speak to him."

"Please, Cheri, sit down." She paused while Cheri sat down in the visitor's chair again. "I knew you were out of his life when I noticed the light in his eyes had died. He threw himself into his job and the ministry. That was his way to compensate for the love he'd lost. For a long time I tried to do the same thing, especially after Stephen married a beautiful blonde green-eyed nurse practitioner." Nadine snickered at the memory. "A few months after Stephen married, I got pregnant with PJ. I thought it would cure all our problems. The day I delivered him, I saw that light back in Preston's eyes. For a moment I had hope, because it seemed our marriage was going to work. And for a time, we had the perfect family."

The phone on Nadine's desk rang. "This is Dr. Owens." She took a breath. "Hello, Dr. Carter." She motioned to Cheri. "I'm sitting here chatting with your appointment. Do you mind if I take a few more minutes? Sure, I don't think she'll mind. I'll walk her over when we're done. Sure. No, thank you."

"I'd better go," Cheri said.

Nadine shook her head and smiled. "You're his last appointment. He's fine with this. Where was I?"

"After PJ you had the perfect family."

"Yes, to the outside world it was perfect. But our hearts weren't in it. Preston was an assistant pastor at the time and we should have called it quits then. It would have alleviated much of the hardship we've gone through, but we struggled to hold things together. It wasn't too long after that that he became pastor. Preston was building a ministry second to none and I worked to become the best general practitioner this side of the northeast. Then one day Stephen stepped into my office and told me he was getting a divorce because of me."

Cheri squint her eyes in confusion.

Nadine smiled when she saw the puzzled look on the other woman's face. "I had that same look when he came to me that day saying, quote unquote, I had broken up his marriage." Nadine shook her head at the memory. "You see, I'd been faithful and I hadn't been intimate with any other man since I married Preston."

"Then, why?" asked Cheri.

"According to him, our being so close in the work environment made it impossible for him to completely sever his feelings for me. The truth of the matter was the tension between us was just too strong to ignore. Even our coworkers could feel the fire."

Cheri nodded her understanding.

"But I had to think about my family, not just my own happiness. So I resisted the attraction and forced myself to ignore what I felt for him. It didn't do much good, because the flame only turned into an inferno." Nadine smiled at Cheri. "Just when the temptation was about to consume me, I went to Stephen and told him I was going to leave in order to put some distance between us. I demanded that he work out things with his wife the same way I was trying to work things out with my husband. Needless to say, it didn't work. I should never have gone to him that day. That's when the infidelity started."

She got up and walked over to the window. "PJ was just a baby, about nine months old. We knew we were wrong and I certainly couldn't break up my family. We tried to stop it, but it was too easy for us to make excuses not to go home. I could always say I had to pull a double shift and Preston never asked questions." She turned and leaned against the windowsill, facing Cheri. "When I got pregnant again, Preston hadn't told me that he'd had his vasectomy the week after PJ was born. So I had no idea he would think the child I was carrying was not his own."

The words echoed in Cheri's mind. Preston had had a vasectomy. If Nadine hadn't been so engrossed in telling her story she would have realized Cheri was completely stunned. *That's why no one could find anything wrong with me, because there is nothing wrong, with me.* It took Cheri a moment to focus back on what Nadine was saying. Fortunately she kept talking, giving Cheri time to recover.

"...he never told me his suspicions until I was almost six months pregnant. Then after that, he had some tests done and the doctor told him it was virtually impossible for him to have fathered the child. Up until that time, I was hoping that it was indeed my husband's baby; but that was how Stephen and I knew Rachel was ours way before the DNA test confirmed it. Preston moved out of the master bedroom long before we received the test results. He let me know we had a marriage in name only."

"Why didn't he say anything about the vasectomy?" Cheri was just thinking out loud, but Nadine assumed the question was for her. "I never asked since I knew the only reason to do that is to be sure no more children are produced."

"I see. He didn't want to risk having illegitimate babies from affairs he was having."

Nadine smiled a little sadly. "No, he just didn't want any more babies with me."

"Well, I would think he'd have his own thing going on without your knowledge, so he did it only to protect himself from ..."

Nadine shook her head. "No, from the day we married until he started seeing you again, there was no other woman, no affairs. He'd had that done way before we started living separate lives in the same house. Believe me, I would have loved to be able to claim that he'd been unfaithful to me. But the truth of the matter is he wasn't."

She came back around her desk and sat down again. "Rachel was just about one when I saw you on television being introduced as the new morning anchor. I knew Preston was going after you as soon as he found out you were back in town. As a matter of fact, that same evening when he came home from work, I told him about your new position. He was clearly surprised and excited all at the same time. I figured he'd get back with you and give me a divorce."

"I only took the job because it was a once-in-a-lifetime opportunity. I never intended to get involved with him."

"Oh, I know. After a few months of you being back in town, I asked him if he'd been able to get in touch with you. He told me that you refused to see him. I even offered to get in touch with you myself so you'd understand our situation, but he told me to stay out of it. He said the one time you did speak with him that you were right when you told him that he was a married man who had no business pursuing you."

"He made it hard for me."

"Well, he actually gave up after you told him that. So I took matters into my own hands and started sending you things—flowers, stuffed animals, candy. I had it all sent in his name."

Cheri's jaw dropped.

"Since you weren't speaking to him at all, it was easy to deceive you. 'Cause if you were talking to him, you'd have found out he hadn't sent you anything. But after a few weeks of that, I was finally able to convince him to start sending them on his own and you got them from both of us. I finally stopped when he stepped up his deliveries. He never knew I aided in bringing you two together."

"Omigod!"

Nadine chuckled. "I know, you didn't have a clue. But I did it for purely selfish reasons. I wanted out of the marriage and you were that way out. When I saw you sitting in the back of the church one day I knew you were breaking down. I asked Preston if he saw you since you left so quickly after the sermon. He told me he'd spoken to you the evening before and that you and he had decided to be friends and friends only."

"That's all we were for a long time," Cheri confirmed.

"Oh, you all had a platonic relationship longer than I wanted it to be. That's one of the reasons why he wouldn't release me from our marriage."

"He said he wanted to wait until the children were older," Cheri said.

Nadine nodded. "And I thought it was a crazy idea."

Cheri half smiled. "He was trying to be honorable."

"So were you, when you attempted to carry on a platonic relationship with the man you loved." She said it with a grin.

Cheri blew out a long sigh. "It worked for a long time."

"Way too long for my taste, but when it changed it was like the air around us started moving again. I thought for sure he'd want a divorce immediately. It was about a year before we finally decided to separate. I know because his whole attitude changed for the better toward everyone. You had him whistling and singing around the house."

"It should never have happened until you divorced and we were married."

Nadine tilted her head to the side. "I never blamed you, Cheri. I'm telling you all this so you can understand why."

Cheri nodded.

"Preston had taken more from me than any man would have taken from any woman. That's why I never held any animosity toward him either. You brought back that light in his eyes and he even treated me more kindly in the house we shared. Everyone who knew him could see the difference in him. He was happy."

"I was jealous of you," Cheri confessed.

"I noticed that when you came to the hospital that day and handed me his clothes in that white plastic hotel bag," Nadine giggled at the memory that Cheri did not find in the least funny. "When you stormed out of the hospital that day I called Preston on his cell phone. I laughed so hard I could hardly breathe." Nadine remembered she was still laughing when he answered his cell phone on the first ring.

"Are you having trouble in paradise, Pastor Owens?"

"What do you want, Nadine?"

"Why are you so testy with me?"

"What do you want?" He demanded.

"I thought you said you were practicing what you preached, hypocrite." She could not resist teasing him.

"If you were a godly woman I wouldn't be..."

"Caught with your pants down, or should I say, off!" Nadine laughed even louder.

"Ha, ha, I guess news travels faster than I thought."

"Your woman just left here. I have your clothes. Do you want me to bring them to you?" she asked jokingly.

"That's not funny. And no, I had Gwen bring me a suit from the church. I'm on my way to the revival now."

"Be sure you repent before you step foot into that pulpit."

"This is your fault, you know."

Nadine stopped laughing. "Oh, it's my fault?"

"Yes, it is," he said accusingly.

"It's my fault that you are tempted by Satan and continue to fail the test, dear heart?" Nadine asked seriously and waited for him to answer.

He cleared his throat and finally choked out, "She wants what I can't give her."

"And what's that?"

He paused, then said, "She wants what you have."

"No, dear heart, she wants what she thinks I have."

"I have to go."

"Preston, all she wants is you."

"Deacon Johnson is flagging at me to get in the church."

"Forget Deacon Johnson, Preston. See that's the problem here, this whole thing is our fault, our fault, Preston, yours and mine. Both of us are to blame for allowing other people to direct our lives."

"You're right. I should have taken your advice years ago and just let the chips fall where they may."

"It would have been better." Nadine responded.

"I see that now," Preston affirmed.

She paused. "Divorce isn't always a bad thing, Preston."

"Yeah, I see that now, too."

Nadine took a deep breath. Preston had just agreed with her. Maybe there was hope to finally end this bogus marriage. "Look, get through the revival and we'll talk about this afterwards. We can fix this so all of us can be happy."

"Tell me how without hurting our children."

"We must reap what we sowed, Preston. The children won't come out of this without wounds. I wish they could. On the flip side, I'm going to assume that you're not worried about the church anymore and ready to resolve this so we can move on with the rest of our lives in the marvelous light?"

"The church is sovereign. It can weather any storm, but the children..."

"I can't stay in this marriage until the children are grown, Preston. We need to divorce. I love Stephen... and don't you love Cheri? Don't you think they're tired of being hidden in the dark?"

He ignored the question and asked her one of his own. "Why did you let me do this, Nadine?"

"Do what? Continue this farce of a marriage?"

"Yeah, you knew you wanted to be with Stephen before we married. If both of us would have stood together and said no, we could have avoided all this."

"I was petrified. I didn't want my family to know what I'd done or how deep the deception was. Anyway, I expected you to denounce me before the congregation and divorce me at once. Why didn't you do that? You had every right to do so."

"You know I couldn't do that, I'd just been installed as pastor of the church. The congregation was growing, but they were babes in Christ and people had confidence in me to take the church to the next level. How could I deliver a blow like that? It would have crippled the very foundation."

"Well, I don't care about other people's opinion of me anymore, and I want a divorce. If you don't file, I will. So get through your revival and then we'll discuss this."

"I thought I was the one who pushed him into a divorce by telling him I was going to marry Curtis Evans," Cheri said, bringing Nadine back to the present.

Nadine smiled. "Oh, he was certainly afraid of losing you. That was probably the straw that broke the camel's back and set us free."

Cheri stood, no longer interested in listening further. "I don't need to see the doctor anymore. Will you let him know I've cancelled?"

Nadine's eyes widened. "Are you sure?"

Cheri had already opened the door and was gone.

Chapter Seven

Cheri felt numb. She had driven from the doctor's office with tears streaming down her face, wondering what she was going to do. To her way of thinking, this was the ultimate betrayal, even worse than the adultery her father had committed that had hurt her mother so badly.

Preston should have told her, but he made the choice to not inform her he had made himself sterile. To let her suffer and question herself.

When she got to Jade and Darrell's house she noticed two extra cars in the driveway. There was no way she could go into the house in her state with company there. So after she parked the car in the garage she remained in it, trying to get her emotions under control. Why in the world didn't he tell me he'd had a vasectomy? She couldn't understand his reasoning. All that time and money had been spent for nothing.

After she sat there a little more than twenty minutes, Darrell drove his car into the garage. She made an effort to look and act normal.

"Hey," Darrell greeted her.

"Hi," she said and forced a smile.

"You need help with anything?" Darrell asked.

"No, I'm just meditating. I'll be into the house in a few minutes," she answered with a shaky voice as she wiped her eyes."

"You sure you're okay?" He scanned her face seeking reassurance.

"Yes," she answered with a crooked smile, not trusting herself to say any more.

Darrell nodded and went into the house. She watched him until he disappeared. Then she buried her face in her hands and broke out in uncontrollable tears again.

The only consolation she felt came from having seen her father today. Before she left his house, they'd agreed to spend the next day together, just the two of them. She had a lot of questions she wanted answers to.

Cheri snapped her head up when she heard the garage door open. Jade came in, opened the car door, and got in, not saying a single word.

Cheri tried to calm herself, but her emotions were too raw to maintain her composure and she began to shake uncontrollably. Jade gasped Cheri's hand in hers. "What's wrong?" Jade asked gently.

Cheri attempted to speak but couldn't. What was she going to say, anyway? What could she say other than the truth?

After a long while Jade said, "The doctor must have had some pretty disturbing news to have you so upset."

"I never saw the doctor," she answered brokenly.

"What do you mean, you haven't seen the doctor?"

"There was no need to."

Jade's eyes widened in surprise after Cheri told her what Nadine had said. "I hate him right now, Jade. Our relationship has been one big drama after the other and I'm sick and tired of it. I don't have anything else to say to him. I just want to restore my relationship with my mother and father and move on with my life."

Jade sighed. "Hate is a pretty strong word."

"Well, it's how I feel right now."

"Sweetie, you may hate the predicament he's put you in, and you may even hate what he did. But you don't hate him and you know it, so talk to him and resolve this."

"I'm so angry with him I don't believe I can have a civil discussion with him."

Jade nodded. "Then let him know that. Don't hide anything from him, just let him have it. Let him know you are really pissed with him. I know what I'm talking about. Before Darrell and I married I kept a lot of stuff from him. Believe me when I tell you, it almost ruined my life."

"I've been open and honest with Preston. He's the one holding secrets, not me!"

"But you didn't tell him you were trying to get pregnant. Maybe if he'd known ..."

Before she could finish, Cheri interrupted her. "He should have told me years ago. There's no excuse for not letting me know what he'd done."

"No, I agree: he should have told you. And you need to tell him that. But don't close the door and walk away without talking about it." Jade took her hand. "He loves you, Cheri. He gave up everything just to be with you. So don't cut off the lines of communication. Give him a chance to explain why he didn't tell you. And look at it this way. The operation was done way before he knew the two of you would marry. So the question is, would you have married him if you knew he'd made himself sterile?" Jade squeezed her hand and Cheri looked at her a little perplexed. "I don't want you to answer. Just think about it."

Cheri's cell phone was vibrating again for the third time. She opened it and closed it quickly.

Jade rubbed her friend's hand. "Come on. Let's go into the house. This can't be fixed by sitting here complaining."

"You have guests and I'd rather not..."

"They left just before I came out here with you. So let's go inside."

ဆၣလ

Two days later Cheri stood at the back door of her mother's home praying she would be allowed to see her. She and her father had spent the entire day together yesterday. Once he told her no subject was off limits, she asked every single thing that had been on her heart since childhood.

And to her amazement, he'd answered every one of them.

Now her mission was to reconcile her relationship with her mother—and maybe even refute or validate some of the information she had gotten from her father.

She tapped on the door a second time before it was finally flung open. "Why are you here?" her sister snapped. "I told you not to come until I called you. I don't know why you insist on upsetting Mama!"

"I don't want to upset her. I just want to see her," Cheri pleaded.

"No." Sandra's voice was cold.

"Just tell her I'm here."

"No."

"Why?"

"Because once you upset her and leave, then I'll have to deal with the aftermath, that's why." She sounded defensive and Cheri wondered why.

"Well, will you just tell her I only want to see her face, she doesn't have to say anything to me. I just want to look at her, and I promise…"

"Let her in, Sandra."

Both women looked in the direction of their mother's voice. Cheri immediately pushed past her sister.

"You sure you're up to this, Mama?" Sandra asked, concerned, following Cheri into the living room.

"I'm fine," she answered as she sat in her favorite recliner.

Cheri noticed she was a little winded from just that short walk. She wanted to hug and kiss her mother's cheek, and under ordinary circumstances her mother would have expected nothing less.

Bernadette quickly sat in the chair, not even glancing at the daughter she hadn't seen in over a year.

Cheri could not believe her good fortune. Her mother had invited her into her home and she silently thanked God for the opportunity.

"You want your oxygen?"

Instead of answering Sandra, Bernadette addressed her youngest child. "Say what you want to say to me."

Cheri knelt in front of her chair and placed her hand on top of her mother's own. "I love you, Mama. I miss you and I'm sorry about everything that's happened between us."

Her mother raised her head, looking directly at Cheri but not saying anything.

Cheri was nervous. "I know you think I'm a home wrecker and a lowlife, but I had nothing to do with Preston's decision to leave his family. I was wrong for having an affair with him. I know that, but God is a forgiving God and I know he's forgiven me. I'm asking you to forgive me too."

There was a lengthy silence. "Is that all you have to say to me?"

"I don't know what else to say, other than I'm sorry and I want you to forgive me." Cheri was sincere and her mother knew without a doubt she wanted to end their quarrel.

"Isn't there anything else you want me to know?" her mother questioned again.

Cheri felt confused. She had no idea what her mother wanted her to say or confess to. She was being as humble as she could be. She was on her knees, yet her mother wanted more? "No. I'm just sorry all this happened the way it did."

Bernadette continued to stare at Cheri. At that very moment, Cheri made up in her mind that she was not leaving this house today without reconciling, so she was ready to confess to just about anything her mother wanted her to in order to make that happen. "Why didn't you tell me Preston's ex-wife had a child with another man while they were married?" Bernadette's voice was rough.

Sandra's sharp intake of breath reminded both women she was still in the room.

Cheri dropped her gaze to their joined hands. "How did you know about that?" Clearly the question had caught her off-guard.

"Never you mind how I found out," her mother admonished her. "Why didn't you tell me?"

"Because that wasn't an excuse for my actions. I knew I was wrong for allowing a relationship to develop between us, so I…"

"If you had told me I would have been able to understand the predicament you were in."

Cheri's eyes widened in surprise.

"I would have counseled you instead of accusing you of being a home wrecker," Bernadette said with remorse. "I really thought you had destroyed that woman's marriage by having an affair with her husband."

"You have to be kidding, Mama," Sandra huffed.

"I didn't think it mattered." Cheri answered her mother honestly, not paying any attention to the expression on her sister's face.

"If I had known the truth, I would have met with you and Preston when you asked me to. I would have understood he'd been provoked into doing what he did. The husband's not the only one who can destroy a marriage through infidelity, a wife can too," Bernadette said.

Cheri could only repeat herself. "I didn't think it mattered."

"She was still wrong!" Sandra's voice was charged with agitation.

Bernadette looked at Sandra sternly. "Get out," she ordered. When Sandra didn't move, she raised her voice. "Right now! This is between your sister and me!"

Bernadette didn't say anything else until Sandra was gone. Directing her attention back to her younger daughter she said gently, "It mattered, Cheri. If you had been open and honest about everything, I would have sat the two of you down and told you to stop seeing each other until Preston had gotten a divorce. I would have planned your wedding myself, sat on the front pew and beamed with pride while the ceremony was being performed."

Omigod, Cheri thought, Mama does have a heart. "I wanted you to hear it from Preston, but you wouldn't talk to him."

"Only because I didn't know the full story and my daughter didn't tell me," she said. "You had the opportunity, but you kept the details from me."

"That was wrong," she admitted after thinking about it for a moment.

"It wasn't the best decision," her mother said in agreement.

"How did you find out?" Cheri really wanted to know the answer.

"A few days ago, the leaders of the Bethany Association came to see me. I've known Bishop Harris a long time and he was with them. They told me that Preston Owens lived with his wife knowing before the child was born that it was not his own. They said Owens came to them with the evidence less than a month after she was born. That was way before you came back here to live. They told me everything, I know the whole story. I know why he stayed with her instead of divorcing that woman from the beginning. They told me they knew when your relationship with Owens started, because he told them that he was actively pursuing you. They said they should have handled it from the beginning, but Owens was worried about the effect on the children." Her mother paused, "I just don't understand why you didn't share information that was that important with me."

"I didn't know it would have made a difference," Cheri answered, mystified.

"Well, now you know," she replied with a sad smile. "It's my understanding that your marriage is fully supported by the association and if Preston wanted to return to the ministry in this area he could."

Cheri shook her head. "That will never happen."

"Never say never, baby. I never thought you and I would ever speak again, but here we are." She smiled. "One of my main worries about this whole thing was I thought that you would never be accepted by the Christian community."

"I never cared about that. I only cared about you and what you thought of me," Cheri answered. "And when you said you never wanted to see me again…"

"I only said what I said as a threat to get you to see things my way," her mother interrupted. "But what I didn't anticipate was that your love for him would be stronger than your love for me."

"Mama, I …"

"Now hold on and let me finish. I understand why you were so unyielding about being with him. I haven't heard of that kind of commitment between a man and a woman since your great-great-grandparents."

Cheri smiled. She knew the story about her white great-great-grandfather all too well. He was the sole heir to a Louisiana plantation that grew indigo, tobacco, sugar, and cotton. Pierre Beauvais forfeited his share of the family fortune to his sister Antoinette after falling in love with her Haitian immigrant great-great-grandmother who was only sixteen years old at the time of their union. Together they had twelve children, three girls and nine boys, which started the Beauvais Creole side of her family.

"I've missed you, Mama." Cheri laid her head on her mother's lap.

"And I've missed you. I owe you an apology. I didn't handle this well at all and I'm sorry. Yesterday, I promised God I'd never play judge and jury ever again."

Cheri's head snapped up. "You really mean that, Mama?"

"I really mean that, baby, never again," her mother confirmed with a smile.

Cheri saw this moment as an opportunity to move to the next phase of her plan. "I spent the day with Daddy, yesterday."

Her mother went still.

"We talked about everything."

There was still no movement.

"I didn't know that you never divorced."

Her mother shut her eyes tightly.

"I've heard his side of the story and I wish you would tell me yours."

There was a pregnant pause before she heard her ask, "What did he tell you happened?"

Cheri said softly, "He said he was unfaithful to you and you kicked him out of the house."

"Is that all he said?"

"No, but first I'd like to hear your side."

Bernadette cleared her throat. "It's true. I forced him to leave. I'd put his clothes in plastic bags and place them outside and he'd bring them right back in the house. That went on for weeks and we argued every day. He slept in your room and you slept with me during that whole time."

"I remember you and him arguing a lot."

"It wasn't always that way. I loved your father," she said with a low voice. "Way too much," she murmured as if it was an afterthought.

Cheri said, "He told me he didn't want to leave, but you wouldn't forgive him. He said he only left when you threatened to have him arrested."

"The woman he was seeing had come to our home while I was at work. You didn't go to school that day because you were ill. Your father stayed with you and you told me that she had come to the house."

Cheri squint her eyes. "I did?"

Her mother nodded. "I confronted your father and he told me she had been there and that he told her to leave and not to come back. I just blew up. I'd never been that angry in my life. I hit him and I kept hitting him until he got mad enough to hit me back. So, when he did, I threatened to press charges against him for domestic violence."

"So he walked away."

Bernadette nodded. "I was never unfaithful to your father. I was hurt and I wanted him to hurt too. So I used the only thing I knew he loved against him."

"You used us?" It was as much a statement as a question.

Her mother didn't answer. She didn't have to.

"Daddy said he wanted to support us, but you wouldn't take anything from him, so at the advice of his attorney he put the money in a bank account. He said when you got in financial trouble with the house Uncle Jerry told him, so he used that money to save our home. Is that true, Mama?"

Her mother nodded.

"Did he leave our Christmas gifts on the porch every year until I went to college?"

"He never forgot any of our birthdays and he sent me flowers every Mother's Day." Bernadette finally looked at her.

Cheri was stunned. When her father had told her all these things she couldn't believe them. No way had her mother purposely separated her and her sister from their father! But she had, and she had told her why. "I was young and foolish. I know I robbed you and Sandra from having a relationship with your father, but there's nothing I can do about it now." She held her head up. "I'm sorry 'bout everything, and that's all I'm saying 'bout that."

"Daddy said he really tried to work things out with you, but you didn't want to work out anything and you…"

"That's all I'm saying 'bout that," she repeated sharply.

Cheri knew the conversation about her father was now over and as the silence stretched between them she saw a tear fall from her mother's left eye.

Cheri shifted her focus on the good that developed today. "I love you, Mama."

"I love you, Cheri, and I want you to forgive me too, okay?"

Cheri nodded, wisely not pushing the issue any further at this time.

Bernadette wiped her eyes with the back of her hand. "I want to plan a reception for you so our whole family can get acquainted with Pastor Owens and his family. For once and for all I want to put this whole thing behind us. So having it as soon as possible would be best."

Cheri blew out a long sigh. "I don't think that's a good idea, Mama."

"Well, why not?"

"I have no relationship with Preston's family. Well, that is, other than his ex-wife and son—and further to that, Preston and I, well... we have some problems, and I don't think they can be solved by having a party."

"What kind of problems?"

"We're not talking right now," Cheri said with an edge of regret.

Her mother batted her eyelashes. "Has he been unfaithful to you?"

"No."

"Does he hit you?"

"No, we don't fight—physically, that is."

"So he's mentally abusive?"

Cheri paused before saying, "He's a liar, Mama."

Her mother crossed her arms. "Can you be more specific?"

Cheri repeated the whole conversation she'd had with Preston's ex-wife to clarify her meaning and her mother listened without interruption. When she finished telling the whole story her mother said. "So, your point is?"

The point was that Cheri wanted sympathy.

Instead of her mother jumping to Cheri's defense, she asked, "If you had known about this when you were dating, would you have stopped seeing him?"

Cheri dropped her chin to her chest. Jade had asked her a similar question.

Her mother smiled. "I don't think you would have," she answered her own question. "You've loved Preston Owens since the day you met him way back in your first year of college. And just like your great-great-grandfather, you were willing to give up your whole family for him. You jeopardized your relationship with me for his love."

"That was wrong too."

Her mother gasped, "Monique Cheri Anderson Owens, don't make this mole hill a mountain. You and Preston will work this out."

"He took away my chance of being a mother," she pouted.

"With today's technology I'm sure there are alternatives. The solution may cost you a small fortune, but I'm sure there's something that can be done."

"I don't understand why he didn't tell me from the very beginning."

"Ask your husband that question."

Cheri shook her head. "I'm so angry with him I don't think I can talk to him at all."

"Well, then wait 'til you cool off. But that's not going to stop me from planning..." She stopped mid-sentence. "Well, now that you've told me all this, I think a rededication ceremony would be in order, immediately followed by the reception."

"Mama, don't plan anything. I don't know what's going to happen now."

Her mother tilted her head to the side. "Do you still love him, Cheri?"

"All I feel is pain, Mama."

"Under those feelings, do you love him?"

Cheri shrugged her shoulders. She was still angry with him.

Her mother patted her hand, stood and walked toward the dining room. She halted at the archway that divided the two rooms. "If you didn't love him, it wouldn't have hurt you so deeply. This wound is new, so you'll need some time for it to heal. Call your husband."

"I can't."

"Yes, you can. I've been saying for years that you're just like your daddy, when in fact you're just like me, stubborn as hell. Learn from my mistakes, baby. Learn how to forgive and move on. Don't follow in my footsteps. Now, I know it couldn't have been easy hearing about the news of his vasectomy from his ex-wife, no less, so just give it time and don't make any hasty decisions." She turned and walked into the kitchen, calling out, "I told Preston last night he had to be patient. You want some juice?"

Cheri twirled around. "You talked to Preston?

Chapter Eight

Preston was worried. Just the thought of losing his wife terrified him. He knew he should have been forthright in telling her he had made the decision to become sterile, but he hadn't—and now he was paying for it. It wasn't as if his decision had anything to do with her, after all. He simply did not want to bring another child in the middle of a loveless marriage.

What was he going to do? Cheri had not accepted a single call from him since talking to Nadine. In the beginning, he had no idea why she would not return his calls. Then Nadine called him about their son, and during that conversation he found out she told Cheri that he had had a vasectomy. At first, he was vexed and blamed Nadine for stirring up trouble by revealing information that he should have revealed himself. But as soon as the accusation fell from his lips, he knew he had no one to fault other than himself.

He had no idea that her trip to New Jersey included an appointment with a fertility doctor that happened to be a colleague of his ex-wife's. According to Nadine and unbeknownst to him, Cheri had seen a few doctors in Alabama. It was no surprise that she wanted a child, especially since she had given him that information on adoption. So now he had to figure out a way to save his marriage. No way was he going to allow his wife to leave him without a fight. He loved her too much for that.

After three days of no communication he was finally able to persuade a reluctant Jade to tell him Cheri was now staying with her mother and had been there since the day they reconciled. So he called his mother-in-law's home, and to his surprise, Bernadette was happy to hear from him. She thanked him for arranging her meeting with the ministers of Bethany, which had made it possible to resolve the feud between her and her daughter.

The truce between them couldn't have come at a better time. Since she was being so honest, he figured he'd do the same and tell her that Cheri was not talking to him and the reason why. To his surprise she was sympathetic and advised him to give her a few days to calm down. That had been four days ago and he was becoming impatient. It was his hope that he could use the newfound alliance between him and his mother-in-law to intervene on his behalf to get his wife to talk to him. What did he have to lose? So he dialed her number.

"Hello?"

He took a deep breath. "Good morning, Mrs. Anderson, this is Preston."

"Good morning. How are you today?"

"I miss my wife." He got straight to the point. "Is she there?"

"No, she went over to the station about a job."

He felt as if she had punched him in the stomach. "She has a job here." He paused. "What is she thinking?"

"Not very clearly, it seems."

"I can't lose her, Mrs. Anderson."

Bernadette shut her eyes tightly. You would have to be a fool not to hear the pain in his voice. Both of them were suffering. There had not been a day that Cheri had not shed tears over their separation. "After all you two have been through, it would be a pity to not finish this race. So when are you coming here to get your wife, son?"

Preston half-smiled at the endearment. "It will have to be next week. I just started a new position, so I can't break free before then. In the meantime, I'll keep trying to get her on her cell phone and on your home number."

"And I'll keep insisting that she call you."

"Thanks, I appreciate that. Enjoy the rest of your day."

"You do the same."

That short conversation made Preston even more uneasy about his future with Cheri. He knew for sure she had no intention of returning to Birmingham without him taking control over this situation. He rubbed the back of his neck, feeling the tension build. He was nervous. He picked up the phone and dialed her cell phone number again. After five rings her voice mail message came on. There was no sense in leaving yet another message. He paused a moment, then dialed another number.

"Hey, Nadine... I need your help."

𝔈𝔊

"Preston again?"

Cheri pressed the mute button and closed her cell phone before nodding in reply to Greg's question.

"You've been here, what?" He looked at his watch. "One hour and he's called you four, five times?"

Cheri shrugged.

"If he's at work, he's not getting very much done." Greg stood to get a book from a shelf in his office. "The

man could lose his job, baby girl, and for what? Over
something stupid."

"It's not stupid to me," Cheri mumbled.

"No, it's silly as hell, that's what it is. It's clear the
man's not concentrating on work because he's
constantly calling you." He shook his head. "I never did
care for that man, because I've seen first-hand how sad
he's made you on more than one occasion. Remember
that argument you had in the parking lot with him?
Remember how you cried yourself to sleep in my
apartment after promising me it was over between you
two, and then you went right back to him? Remember?"

"That was then, this is now."

"Yeah, well, and from what you've told me, he's not
a complete jackass. So I'm a forgiving guy." Greg
dropped the book on his desk. "Why won't you talk to
him?"

Cheri stood up. "I'm sorry I shouldn't have come to
you with all this."

"Sit your ass down. That's your problem: you're
always running when things get uncomfortable.

Cheri glared at him.

"I'm not scared of you, sit down, now. We're going
to talk about this whether you like it or not. You and I
have always been close. I'm four years older than you,
but it was you who helped me get over a horrible
marriage to an unfaithful wife by letting me move a bed
in your office space in your tiny apartment in Brooklyn
when I didn't have no place to go. You fed me when I
was a broke student in law school when we lived in the
same apartment building in Jersey. I probably know
you better than anyone in our whole family. For sure I
was the only one who knew about your affair with
Pastor Owens, cause you never told anybody but me.

"Curtis Evans knew."

"Curtis wasn't family, though he wanted to be."

Cheri shook her head. "He just wanted me to be happy."

"The man was in love with you, Cheri, but all you could see was Preston Owens. I know, because he confessed to me just how he felt about you."

"You don't know what you're talking about. We were the best of friends."

"He was in love with you and he's still in love with you. But after you married Owens he knew it was over. He left here brokenhearted, but you couldn't see that. You were too busy basking in the euphoria of your new marriage."

"He never said anything."

"That's because he wanted you to know it through his actions. That's why he asked you to marry him when you and Preston broke up those few months. He wanted to share a house with you, have babies with you, and spend the rest of his life with you. He told me he was going to be so good to you that you wouldn't have any other recourse but to fall in love with him. I told him he was crazy. I told him he was setting himself up for heartbreak, but he wouldn't listen to me."

Cheri had not heard from Curtis since she'd married Preston. She thought it was because she had moved to Birmingham and he had gone to Chicago.

"Since the day you met Preston Owens, I haven't heard you once talk about being interested in another dude. Even during the years you weren't seeing him, I can't remember one single guy you dated—other than Curtis, who I don't even count, since to you he was more like a cousin. But now, just because Owens didn't tell you about a procedure he had performed during those years of hiatus, you want to move back here and write the whole marriage off! Woman, have you lost your mind?"

"I didn't say that."

"Then what are you saying?"

"I need time to think about all this. I just want to be alone for a while, that's all." She knew she sounded resentful.

"You just remember, while you're thinking, when you married him you made the decision to not be alone anymore until death do you part. You decided to be one with him. He's your husband. Even the church and state recognize that."

Later that week she was still remembering the conversation. Greg had been right. Though her dates were sporadic during her separation, she'd never allowed herself to become involved with any of the men she'd met. She really had thought about spending the rest of her life with Curtis: she loved him, but she was never in love with him.

They hung out together and she confided in him. They shared a genuine friendship and he knew all too well about her obsession with Preston. For the time she and Preston broke up, it was Curtis who consoled her. He was even willing to marry her and give her as many babies as she wanted. What she hadn't known until that day in her cousin's office was that Curtis had been secretly in love with her.

Soon after Cheri married Preston, Curtis moved to Chicago to take a job as a professor at a university, and she and Preston started a new life in Birmingham. Since then, she has only spoken to Curtis twice by telephone.

Cheri raised her eyes toward the door after hearing a tap. "It's not locked." she called out.

Sandra pushed the door open. "Can I come in?"

"Sure." Cheri wiped the lone tear from her face, attempting to hide it.

Her sister sat on the bed next to her, took the book from her lap and read the front cover. "A Matter of Time, a novel by Reign."

"It's a good book."

She flipped the book over to read the back cover. "Oh, no, it's a love story. I hate love stories. You only get happy endings in a storybook, never in real life."

"That's your opinion."

Sandra laid the book on her lap. "Did you find a place to live yet?"

Cheri hunched her shoulders. "I think so."

"Well, I'm going to hate to see you go back to Alabama, but I understand, since you already have a job there."

Cheri simply nodded.

"So when are you leaving?"

"Next weekend. I have to be back to work on the first. They're giving me the early morning anchor position."

"Wow, that's great news! When did you find out?"

Cheri smiled. "Yesterday. The director called and told me that Jay took a job in Dallas and so they want to move me to the early morning news. So I accepted."

"Well, now you can really afford that apartment you were looking at on the internet. It does pay more, right?"

"Absolutely."

Her sister nudged her shoulder, "Congrats, little sis!"

"Thanks."

"I'd like to come out there during the summer and see what it's like. Maybe even find a job there. I'd like to relocate someplace else. I'm tired of Jersey."

"I don't think you're ready for the slower pace of a southern city."

"Is it Green-Acres slow?"

"I've never been there, so I don't know. But it's almost too slow for me, and you know what a bore I am."

"Now that you mention it, I've noticed you've slowed your pace."

Cheri laughed. "Well, try it, you might like it."

"Anyway, I'm going to a movie, get a bite to eat, have simulating conversation with a few friends. I thought you might like to join us."

Cheri took the book back from her. "No, thank you."

Sandra pouted. "Come on, Cheri. You've been in this room day in and day out. I know you're depressed, 'cause you're not eating. You'll never get over that man if you keep moping around in this room. So come on and hang out with your big sister."

"No, you go and have enough fun for both of us. I'm going to finish my book."

Sandra's son burst into the room. "Aunt Cheri, Gram said come downstairs, right now!"

"Saved by your mother!" Sandra called out to Cheri's retreating back.

As soon as Cheri's feet hit the bottom step, she heard Preston's voice. "I was lucky and was able to get an earlier flight," he was saying to her mother.

"Here she is," Bernadette exclaimed as Cheri came into the room.

"What are you doing here?" Cheri asked mechanically.

Preston quickly crossed the room, took her by the hand and kissed her cheek. "I've missed you," he whispered in her ear as he hugged her tightly.

"You need privacy, so I'll be in the kitchen." Bernadette excused herself and left them alone.

Preston held her. "Why haven't you returned my calls?"

Cheri answered, meeting his eyes. "Obviously I didn't want to speak to you."

"We'll never resolve anything by not talking, darling. Come," he beckoned, "let's sit down." He moved to the sofa.

"I'd rather stand, thank you."

"I rather you not, I want to look into your eyes while we're talking." He patted the cushion next to him.

Cheri pushed her hair from her forehead then took the chair opposite him.

He smiled at her rebellious nature. "Afraid to be too close to me, darling?"

"What do you want, Preston?"

He crossed his leg over his knee. "I want to take you home."

She glared at him. "I want an explanation."

Preston sighed. "I never lied to you, but you lied to me."

"What did I lie about?" she asked defensively.

"The reason you left your ticket open when you purchased it."

"I did not lie to you," she said, shaking her head.

"Yes you did. Let me remind you of the conversation we had. Remember I asked you, 'Why didn't you get a return ticket?' And you said, 'I have a return ticket, it's just open.' Remember saying that?"

Cheri crossed her arms over her chest.

"I asked you how long you were staying and you told me one week," Preston reminded her.

"I changed my mind," Cheri answered.

"Without informing me?"

"Like I'm the only one who doesn't communicate important information?" Cheri snapped.

"This was going to be our week to spend together, remember? I had planned a really nice mini-vacation for us. So when you changed your plans, it messed up my plans for us to spend some quality time together. So, since you seem to have lost your way back home, I've come to escort you."

Both of them turned in the direction of the front door when it opened.

"I'm not helping you the next time, Brian," Cheri's niece Kelly was saying to her brother as they came into the house.

Cheri and Preston both stood up.

"Oh, sorry, Aunt Cheri, I didn't know you had company."

Preston extended his hand to introduce himself to the teenagers.

"So you're our uncle?" Kelly asked.

"If you're Cheri's niece and nephew, then I'm your uncle."

Kelly smiled. "Well, you don't look like a low-down weasel."

Brian nudged his sister, but Preston was smiling. "That's okay, Brian. I've been called worse."

"You two get upstairs and start your homework." Bernadette's voice wafted out of the kitchen.

"Gram, it's Friday, no homework on the weekends," Kelly said with glee.

Bernadette poked her head out of the kitchen and pointed to the stairs. "Get out. Grown folks are talking."

"Preston and I can finish our conversation elsewhere, Mama, so don't run the kids off." Cheri turned to Preston. "Give me a few minutes to change my clothes."

Chapter Nine

Preston sat across from Cheri at the trendy restaurant, wondering why she'd chosen this location. He had wanted to go back to his hotel room to discuss their predicament privately, but she was insistent on coming to this extremely crowded place. She had refused to discuss anything during their drive there, so with the exception of giving directions to the restaurant, she'd been quiet.

She ordered a glass of moscato and he wondered when she'd started drinking wine. She smiled and he could hardly breathe, thinking about what message she held behind that grin.

"You're drinking wine? Are you trying to ease your nervousness or something?"

"No. I tried it for the first time last week while I was out with Sandra and I really liked it. Why don't you try it?"

"No, thank you. It seems to me I need to remain fully alert and attentive for whatever your reason is for bringing me here." He took his handkerchief from his inside pocket and wiped the perspiration from his brow.

"Relax, Preston. Have a glass of wine." She signaled for the waiter.

"No, one of us needs to be sober to drive."

"Yes, miss?" the waiter asked.

"Can you bring out the whole bottle and a glass for my husband, please?"

"That won't be necessary," Preston refused politely.

"It's all right, no one cares if you have a glass of wine," she countered.

"No," he said with finality.

Cheri directed her attention to the waiter. "Never mind."

"As you wish, miss."

"So, now you're drinking?"

"I wouldn't constitute a glass of wine as drinking."

Preston dropped his gaze to his wife's wine glass. He didn't want to argue, he'd come here to take her home, and that was his main objective. He rubbed his left temple feeling a headache coming on. Had this situation bothered her to the point that she felt she needed an alcoholic beverage? He raised his head and glared at her as she picked up a slice of French bread and buttered it.

Then it occurred to him. "You brought me here so I can't make a scene?"

She looked up at him before swallowing the bread she had been chewing. "I wanted to come here because I'm hungry."

He frowned at her and she never broke contact with his eyes. "I'm glad to see your appetite has picked up, because you can't afford to lose another ounce."

Cheri smiled.

"But I'm not giving it to you," he announced firmly.

She leaned forward. "Giving me what, Preston?"

She waited a full minute before he replied, "A divorce."

She continued to stare at him before she broke out in laughter.

"I'm not playing, Cheri. I'm won't allow it," he said hotly.

She laughed even harder. "Is that what you think? That's why you're sweating?"

"I saw the cancelled check you wrote to the apartment complex on the bank's website. I saw what you wrote in the memo, application fee."

Cheri's laughter subsided immediately.

"That's why I'm here, isn't it? That's why you're drinking so you can work up enough courage to tell me you want out of our marriage, right?"

Cheri knew she had to be honest with her husband. "I agree that the evidence points that way," she answered softly.

"Yeah, well, you can forget it!"

"Preston..."

"I'm not giving you up, so I'm telling you, you may as well forget it. You're not getting a divorce!"

She took a sip of wine, all the while boldly holding his gaze. "I thought about a divorce several times," she admitted. Then she placed the glass on the table in front of her. "But just the thought of living the rest of my life without you, even for a moment, depressed the hell out of me."

His lip curled into a slow smile and he broke contact with her eyes for the first time. She could tell he was relieved. "The crazy thing is... I love you, Preston, so in the end, the love I have for you wins."

"Look..."

She held up her hand, stopping his words. "I've always wanted what you've never been able to give me. I wanted it before we were married and I still want it now. The question is would I have married you in spite of the fact that you can't give me a child?" She paused. "And the answer is yes, I would have married you anyway." She took another sip of wine before continuing. "Greg made me see that. He said I've never dated or wanted anyone but you, and he's right. But I think I can still get the desires of my heart by using in vitro fertilization."

"Cheri…"

"Please let me finish. I only want one child of my own. That's all I'm asking, just one. You have PJ, so I know this isn't important to you, but for me it's a lot."

He reached across the table and took both her hands. "If it's important to you, it's important to me too. I want you happy, babe. So you can have as many babies as you want." Preston saw her eyes light up immediately. "You mean that?"

"With all my heart." He was sincere.

"Oh, thank God. I'm really tired of fighting and being upset with you about this." She leaned over the table for a kiss and he met her more than halfway.

"I love to see you smile." He caressed her cheek with the back of his hand.

"Thank you, baby, thank you so very much." She patted the top of his hand. "Your hands are hot," she noticed. "Are you feeling all right?"

He nodded.

"Stop worrying, we're going to work this out. Loosen up, okay?"

Preston relaxed his shoulders. "Okay."

She smiled at his effort. "I have an appointment tomorrow, and I want you to go with me since you're here. We may get to choose a sperm donor!"

He moved his hand away from her. "No," he said. "I'm not allowing another man to get you pregnant."

"It's not anything physical."

"Oh, that's very physical, sweetheart," Preston commented as the waiter came and placed salads in front of them momentarily halting their conversation.

"More wine, miss?"

"Yes, please. Looks like I'm going to need it."

As soon as the waiter finished serving them, Cheri declared in a husky whisper. "It's not like I'm going to lie with the man. It's in a tube, for goodness' sake."

"Doesn't matter how it is. I'm the only man whose sperm has been inside you and that's the way it'll remain. So if you conceive, it will be God's will and my offspring," he retorted, then speared a cucumber and placed it in his mouth.

Cheri could not believe what she was hearing. She shook her head. "I'm not going to argue with you about this," she replied, pushing her salad plate away from her.

"Good. Now that I've had the operation reversed we're going to pray that God moves quickly. In the meantime, I'm going to enjoy focusing all my efforts on knocking you up!"

She stared at him for a moment to digest the meaning of his statement. "You had the vasectomy reversed?"

He nodded. "A week ago."

Her jaw dropped. "So it wasn't permanent?"

He pierced a slice of tomato. "No."

"Why didn't you tell me?"

"You weren't talking to me, remember?"

She was nonplussed. "When did you have time to have it done? Who cared for you while…"

"It's done," he interrupted. No way was he going to tell her that his ex-wife helped him expedite the surgery. "We're not going to talk about it anymore. We just need to get busy, creating."

Preston signaled for the waiter who quickly approached the table.

"Yes sir?"

"Will you remove the wine and bring my wife a glass of club soda with a twist of lime?"

The waiter nodded.

ಲ೦೮೩

"So you're going back to Alabama with him?" Sandra asked. She couldn't quite believe the complete turnaround in her sister's plans.

"Yes, we've decided to work things out."

Sandra shook her head. "You are so gullible. He's always been able to manipulate you."

Cheri spun around to look at her. "What are you talking about?"

"You've always given him his way. When he says jump, you don't even ask how high, you simply start jumping, then you ask is this high enough?" Sandra was being sarcastic.

Cheri refused to be baited by her sister. Especially since she was feeling better than she had in months, her marriage was coming back together, and her chances of conceiving a child were no longer zero. She was going home. There she could finally have the peace and serenity she'd had before PJ came to live with them. "That's not true," Cheri countered.

"Yes, it is. You turned your back on your whole family just to marry him. Then after he lies to you about…"

Cheri swung around again and spoke hotly. "He didn't lie to me! He just neglected to tell me!"

"Same difference! Look at you, you fell for his idiotic explanation."

Cheri placed her hand on her hip, "I'm moving forward in my marriage. I love my husband and I'm learning to be quicker to forgive, especially when he asks me for it. No one is perfect. Not you, or me, our mother or our earthly father, so since he wants to be forgiven, I'm learning to forgive.

"He's making a fool of you," Sandra responded.

Cheri zipped her bag and sat it on the floor. "I'm a happy fool. Are you happy and wise, Sandra?"

"Damn right I'm happy and wise."

"Well your mother isn't. I've talked to her. She knows she made a mistake. She told me she should have forgiven our father years ago. But because she wouldn't is the reason why they've been separated all these years."

"He left her for another woman."

Cheri shook her head. "Mama forced him out of this house!"

"He has children younger than us, Cheri."

"Yes, he does," Cheri agreed, before adding, "I've met our brother!"

Sandra eyes grow wide with surprise. "What?"

Cheri lifted her head with pride. "I've met our brother, his wife, and their son Bradford. We're all grown now and I'm staying in contact with them. They were excited about meeting me and I was glad to meet them."

Sandra squinted. "When did all this take place?"

"After Mama and I talked some days ago about this whole thing, I got in touch with our father and brother and we met at the Four Seasons."

"Half-brother," Sandra grumbled. "I can't believe you would betray our mother that way."

"Oh, don't be so melodramatic. The only reason we didn't have a relationship with our father is because Mama didn't allow us to. The sad part is my instinct told me to contact him years ago and I didn't because of loyalty to Mama. I lost years with my father because I didn't trust my intuition."

"He walked out on us and never looked back."

"He made a mistake and he just didn't know how to fix it," Cheri countered.

"So he mistakenly found himself laid up with another woman?" Sandra responded sarcastically.

"He admitted he was wrong. He knew he was wrong, but he didn't want to lose his family over it. So he stopped seeing her, got an apartment, and begged Mama to forgive him." Cheri took a deep breath. "But she wouldn't, and the woman he and Mama broke up over wasn't the woman he had the children with. He met her after he and Mama split up." Cheri blew out a long sigh. "I have nothing against our half brother, neither should you. We were victims of circumstances."

Sandra leaned against the dresser as if the wind had been knocked out of her. "He hurt our mother," she said stubbornly.

"I know he did, but at some point you have to let it go, Sandra, or the bitterness with eat you alive."

Sandra folded her arms across her chest, contemplating what her sister said.

"Did you know that they never divorced?" Cheri added.

Sandra looked at her sister, perplexed.

"See! Just like me, you didn't know. And like me, you never knew he paid child support."

"Liar!" Sandra accused.

"It's true, he paid monthly and Mama didn't want anything from him. She told him she'd take care of her own children."

"That's a lie!" She was almost shouting.

"At the advice of his attorney, Daddy put the money in a bank account for years. When Mama got behind in the mortgage and the mortgage company contacted him, he took the money from that account and saved our home."

Sandra shook her head. "You're a liar," she insisted.

Cheri glared at her. "Talk to your mother, since she's the only one you'll believe." She walked out of the room, leaving her sister standing with her mouth ajar. Cheri made her way down the stairs to where her mother stood.

"I enjoyed you being here, baby," her mother said and hugged her. "I'll have a talk with your sister."

Cheri leaned back to look into her mother's eyes. "Thank you, Mama."

"When are you leaving?" Bernadette asked Preston.

"Tomorrow morning, our flight leaves at six-fifteen."

"Then why are you leaving now?" her mother asked.

"We're spending the day with my parents. I think a talk with them is long overdue," Preston answered. He reached for the luggage Cheri brought down and swayed.

"Hey, you okay?" Bernadette asked.

"I'm fine. Just tired, that's all."

"Well, you'll be able to sleep now that you're taking your wife home!"

Preston smiled in agreement.

"To be honest, I'm not looking forward to spending time with his parents," Cheri complained to her mother.

"Well, if the ministers visited them as they did me. I'm sure things are going to be just fine," her mother responded.

"I don't know about that. They've never liked me."

"You stay as sweet as you are, and they'll come around."

***

"Would you like something to drink, Cheri?" Preston's mother was being overly pleasant.

Cheri was extremely formal. "No, thank you, Mrs. Owens."

Preston had his guard up, knowing just how offensive his father could be.

Bishop Owens was totally indifferent. "So, son, I understand that you may have a position in Alabama as assistant pastor."

Preston was astonished by the comment, since he hadn't shared that information openly. "What?"

"Don't be so surprised, you knew Bishop Taylor would tell me that the pastor in Birmingham is looking at you," Preston's father responded.

"Well, I'm not really thinking about that right now. I just started a new position with the state and Cheri will be anchoring the morning news in a few weeks."

"That's not more important than God's business."

"Dad…"

"I have some homemade carrot cake," Mrs. Owens announced, wisely stopping the argument before it started. "Would you like some, Cheri?"

"No, thank you." She declined politely with a smile.

"Preston?" she called to get his attention. "What about you?"

"You know your carrot cake is one of my favorites, Mother. I want a huge slice.

She looked at her husband. "None for me," Preston's father answered.

Cheri had no idea about the assistant pastor position. How could she: she'd cut off all communication with Preston for the last few weeks, and they had not had much time to discuss much since the feud ended.

"Dad, you have to understand that at this moment, I'm more concerned about my family. If I can't run my own house, how can I run God's house?"

"It's only an assistant position, so you won't have full responsibility of the church. So I can't see how it will be a hindrance."

"Look, I really don't want to talk about the ministry right now, Dad. Let's just enjoy each other's company, what about that?"

After a few moments of silence Cheri stood up. "I'll see if your mother needs any help."

"This is nonsense," Preston's father announced before Cheri had a chance to leave the room. "You come in here acting like nothing is wrong, and I just found out that the child I thought was my granddaughter isn't. What did you do to drive that girl into the arms of another man?"

At that very moment, Preston's mother reentered the room with a huge slice of carrot cake in hand. Preston looked to her with a pleading expression. "Mother…"

"Charles," she called as a warning, handing Cheri the plate of cake.

"I just want to know what happened, and I want the truth. Did your affair with her cause this fiasco?" He asked pointing at Cheri.

Cheri gave Preston the cake without sitting down: she was ready to leave. She knew where this was going and she refused to be insulted by this hypocrite. "Sit down, sweetie," Mrs. Owens spoke gently to Cheri. When she did not move, the older woman added, "please?"

Cheri sat down beside her husband. Preston set the cake on the table next to his seat without tasting it and took his wife's hand in his. Cheri noticed his hand was awfully warm and sweaty. His father had surely shaken him up, for him to have this kind of reaction. She immediately shut her eyes tightly and said a silent prayer. Lord in the name of your son Jesus Christ, please don't allow me to snap, because if that man says another thing about me or to me, I just might slap the taste out of his mouth. So I'm asking you, Lord, help me hold my peace so you can fight my battle.

"Charles, that's enough," Mrs. Owens admonished her husband. "Now, we are all hurt by the news that Nadine's daughter is not our grandchild, but there's no sense in getting on Preston for Nadine's behavior."

"She didn't do it for just any old reason," Charles said to his wife.

Please Lord, please help me stay calm and help me stay respectful, because I really don't want to tell this man off in his own house.

"No, she didn't. She did it because she's in love with someone else," Mrs. Owens said with her hand on her hip.

Lord, my husband is shaking. Please give him peace in the mist of this storm. Let him know you have his back.

Preston released Cheri's hand to rub his eyes. She could tell his parents' bantering was really annoying him.

I'm thanking you in advance for the victory, Lord. In Jesus name I pray, Amen.

"I've known Nadine since she was a baby."

"Yes, and we've known Preston since birth, but it doesn't make us know what he's thinking or how he feels in his heart."

He turned to his son. "Did this all start when she found out about you and Cheri?" he asked again.

"Dad, Cheri had nothing to do with any of this," Preston said.

"How can you say that when you brought her to this very house before you married Nadine, and told us you wanted to marry her instead of Nadine?"

"Yes, he did, and we should have listened, Charles," his mother answered for him.

Cheri leaned toward her husband. "Let's get out of here," she whispered. He answered her by threading his fingers through hers giving her hand an assuring squeeze.

"Now, I'm going to tell you what I know." Preston's mother continued. "Nadine came to me and told me all about her affair with an intern she'd met. I told her she's already admitted it, so all she had to do was quit it and forget it. I know now I was wrong for telling her that. I was selfish I never took her feelings into consideration. She cried and cried while telling me she loved Preston like a brother, but not like a woman should love a man and I had the audacity to ignore her plea. I was wrong."

"Mother, you knew, and didn't say anything?" Preston was astounded.

No, not a word, I kept it to myself and instructed her to do the same. I told her things would be fine and she would learn to love you as her husband just like I learned to love your father."

Cheri raised her head to look at Mrs. Owens because she could not believe what her ears just heard. Was she really saying she didn't love her husband when she married him?

"What are you talking about? You knew she was being unfaithful?" Bishop Owens asked.

Cheri thought he either knew that his wife had not loved him when they married or he just wasn't paying attention to exactly what she'd just said.

"I knew before that child was conceived that Nadine was having an affair."

"How did you know, Mother?"

"When I went on that five-day cruise to the Bahamas with Denise and Karen, Nadine was on that same ship, accompanied by Rachel's father."

"You never said anything about seeing her." Preston's father was angry.

"I didn't want to upset my son, and I certainly didn't want to hurt him, that's why I didn't say anything. Nadine and I had some harsh words and I swore Denise and Karen to secrecy."

"Della, you could've told me!" Preston's father exclaimed.

"No, Charles, I couldn't. I've kept a lot of things from you because you're so old-fashioned. Over the years I've learned that you can't judge a book by its cover or where it comes from." She turned to Cheri. "You continue to make my son happy. He deserves to be happy, you hear me?"

"Yes, ma'am."

"And don't call me Mrs. Owens anymore. Call me Mother, just like Preston does. You're the future mother of my grandchildren, so how will it look if their mother is calling their grandmother Mrs. Owens?"

Cheri smiled and placed her hand back in Preston's. She noticed how sweaty his palm still was, and that his face was flushed. "You all right?" she asked in a whisper.

He nodded without looking at her.

His parents were still going at it. "I don't believe you, woman! You made no effort to tell me the truth so the relationship between our son and us could have been mended. I've been upset with him all this time for absolutely nothing," Preston's father bellowed.

"I never stopped talking to our son. I just didn't let you know I spoke to him weekly, sometimes more."

Preston's father gasped. "What?"

"Mother, you know you could have told me what you knew after we divorced," Preston said.

"For what? It was over and I was glad it was over. Do you know when you divorced and married Cheri I was able to sleep at night? I knew then that you were finally with your soul mate."

"I didn't know you'd stop sharing stuff with me, Della." Preston's father was mystified. "We used to always talk, especially at bedtime."

"Well, for the last few years you hop into bed and fall asleep so fast I don't get a chance to talk to you about anything!"

"Does he still snore, Mother?" Preston asked to lighten the mood.

"So loud that his teeth rattle," she answered jokingly, following her son's lead.

"Ouch, Mother, now that's just wrong!"

"Yeah, but it's true!"

All of them laughed except Bishop Owens.

Della came to where her husband was sitting and caressed his face. He was pouting.

"Cheri is Preston's wife, Charles. Just like I'm yours and we need to respect them. That's the godly thing to do, don't you think?"

Charles nodded.

Cheri touched Preston's face, then his forehead. "You have a fever," she told him.

"I'm all right."

"Now all this other stuff that's happened between us needs to be buried so we can start over again," Preston's mother proclaimed.

"Amen." Preston agreed.

She turned to Cheri who was still worried about Preston. "Your mother told me about a rededication service she's planning for you and my son, and our family will fully participate," she said, glancing at her husband. "She's going to ask Bishop Taylor to officiate and I'm in full agreement with that. What do you think, honey?"

"Whatever you all do is fine, seems like I had this whole thing figured wrong in the first place."

"Good. Cheri, what do you think?"

"I think we need to take my husband to the hospital.

Chapter Ten

Preston was disoriented.

When he opened his eyes, the first thing he recognized was the medical monitoring equipment. It was confirmation that he was indeed in the hospital. He remembered walking in with his wife and parents. It had taken them almost a half-hour to convince him to seek medical attention, and when he finally agreed and they reached the hospital, it was so crowded that he wanted to leave. But Cheri reminded him that the old-fashioned glass thermometer his mother had used to take his temperature registered one hundred and one, and that convinced him to stay.

"A person could die sitting right here waiting to be seen," he remembered complaining to his wife.

Cheri threaded her fingers through his and he heard her say, "Your father's up at the window now to see how much longer it will be."

After that, he could not remember a thing.

When he boarded that plane on Friday, he knew he was not feeling well. However, nothing was more important than going to New Jersey to persuade his wife to come home. With his eyes wide opened he slowly turned his head and… there she was. He smiled.

Even though Cheri was weary, having slept very little while sitting in a chair next to Preston's bed, her eyes sparkled with joy when he turned his head in her direction and gazed into her eyes. "Hey, you," she murmured.

Seeing her was calming. "Hey," he whispered.

She ran her fingers over his forehead. "You scared us."

"Sorry."

Cheri kissed his lips and caressed his cheek. "You know your mother and father are too old for this kind of excitement."

"What happened?" He felt lethargic.

"You don't remember?"

"I remember being in the lobby waiting a long time and you gripped my hand real tight."

"I grasped your hand when I saw your eyes turned glassy. Then you stopped talking and simply stared. I thought you were having a stroke."

"But I didn't?"

"No, after they examined you thoroughly they told us your body's temperature was so high it caused a seizure."

He shut his eyes for a long moment. "That procedure I had last week caused this."

Cheri shook her head. "I assumed that too, but according to three doctors, no infection or any other problem was found with the surgery."

"So what is it?"

"No one knows. There was nothing in your blood work or the body scan they did. I'm going to assume your father prayed a prayer of protection and restoration so powerful that whatever was wrong, God fixed it."

"If my father can't do anything else, he can pray."

Cheri smiled. "He sure can," she said. "Practically everyone in the emergency waiting room felt the anointing. I could have sworn I saw angels surround us while I sat on the floor with your head in my lap."

He imagined the scene.

"When they first took you to the treatment room, they wouldn't let us go with you, so your father kept right on praying. People he didn't even know started coming up to him for prayer for themselves and others."

Preston smiled.

"It turned into a mini revival," she added jokingly.

"I need to call my job," Preston said, his voice slurring slightly.

"Your doctor sent a letter to personnel first thing this morning. So don't worry about anything."

"And you?"

"The station knows everything. They even sent well-wishes to you." She pointed to the flowers.

He smiled. "My folks?"

"The doctor persuaded them to go home around two this morning, but only after assuring them that you sleeping in a coma-like state was normal after a grand mal seizure."

"I feel drained."

Cheri nodded. "But you're going to be fine."

Preston could tell she was exhausted. "How long you been here?"

She looked at her watch. "About sixteen hours. You slept twelve hours straight."

A soft knock on the door got both of their attention. "Good morning, Mrs. Owens," the doctor greeted her as he entered the room.

"Dr. Clark."

"So you finally woke up!" he said to Preston.

Preston shook his hand and nodded. "Doctor."

"How are you feeling?"

"Exhausted," he said and tried raising his head so Cheri adjusted his pillow.

The doctor flipped through the papers attached to his clipboard. "Other than tired, do you feel anything else, any pain anywhere?"

"No pain, just a little sore."

"Well, that's to be expected. Any other symptoms?"

"No."

"Have you felt differently in the past few days?"

"I haven't been sleeping and I just thought I was fatigued."

"How long haven't you been able to sleep?"

"Since my wife came here to visit her mother about ten days ago," he answered honestly.

"Well, I'm going to order some other tests. If they come out all right, I'll release you in the morning. Now do either of you have any other questions for me?" He looked from Preston to Cheri.

"Can he have something to eat?" Cheri asked.

"Not until after they take some more blood for testing. Anything else?"

"No. Thank you, doctor." Cheri nodded, satisfied.

When the doctor was leaving Preston's parents were just coming in.

ⵠⵣ

Preston was released the following day under advisement not to travel for a few days. So they decided to stay in New Jersey to allow him some additional time to recuperate. Cheri made plans to return to her mother's house. However, when Preston's parents arrived at the hospital around noon they were told that Preston's old room had been prepared for their extended stay. Immediately, Cheri became distraught. No way did she want to stay at her in-laws' home!

"Mrs. Owens…"

"Mother, I told you to call me Mother. That's exactly what Preston has called me all his life."

"Sorry. It's just that... well you see... I... I already made arrangements with my mother to..."

"I spoke to your mother this morning. She's fine with the change in plans."

"Mrs... I mean..."

"Cheri, I understand your apprehension. We didn't get off to a very good start. But my son loves you and I love my son and I'm sure with time my husband and I will get to know you and love you too. So let's look at this whole event as God's way of provoking us into his will."

"I'm sure you and I can, but your husband..."

"I'll make certain that he minds his manners. He may be the head, but I'm the neck, and so I'm able to control the head."

Cheri gave her a half-smile.

"Don't worry. It's going to be fine." She narrowed her eyes at Cheri. "I see now that I'm going to have to teach you how to fight diplomatically." She smiled, turned and started out of the room with one of Preston's bags. "That's the only way you'll be able to survive in this family."

Many of Preston's old parishioners visited him at his parent's home following his release from the hospital. It was soothing to his ego to find out he was still loved by so many and had indeed been missed. Some of them reminded him of sermons he'd preached that affected them both spiritually and physically. They brought food, fruit, flowers, candy, and crossword puzzles so he wouldn't get bored sitting at home recuperating. It had been wonderful and Preston was thankful to the new pastor of Greater Mount Hope Baptist Church, Rev. Dr.

Darrell Parker Jr., for igniting the flame to get this overwhelming response from the people.

Pastor Parker stood before a meeting and told the congregation that only God had a heaven or hell to send anyone to, and in order to be Christ-like, we must learn how to be forgiving. He also told them the truth about why their former pastor had resigned and moved to another state. Preston's former secretary Gwen had already told the truth to her closest friends, so none of the information given by Pastor Parker was news to them. But the ones who did not have an iota of information about anything were surprised to learn about their former First Lady's infidelity.

PJ arrived at his grandmother's house the afternoon Preston was released. Preston's father drove him to and from school so he could be with his father daily. Both PJ and her father-in-law were civil toward her. Cheri assumed that her mother-in-law did indeed have control over the head. During Cheri and Preston's stay it became evident that the in-laws were not as bougie as she'd thought they were, but more down-to-earth. By day three she was feeling more comfortable staying with them, helping her mother-in-law with the meal preparation, household chores, and caring for Preston.

On the evening before she and Preston left for Alabama, she spied a tender exchange between her in-laws that allowed her to see the affection they truly had for each other. Preston's mother was standing near the stove attending to dinner when his father grasped her arm and pulled her onto his lap. She hadn't heard what he said in her ear but she heard her say, "You're wicked, Charles. Too wicked for words and I love you." She kissed her husband with affection as he patted and rubbed her hip.

Cheri intended to back away from the exchange, attempting to keep it private, when she bumped into Preston who was heading to the kitchen for a snack before dinner.

"What's up with you?"

"Hush, your parents are having a private moment," she said as she turned to retreat to another room.

"What are you talking about?" Preston grabbed her by the hand and entered the kitchen. "Oh, that's what you're calling a private moment?" he asked, pointing to his parents who were hugging on a kitchen chair.

Cheri expected them to move away from each other, but instead his mother giggled like a schoolgirl. She grinned, noting that Preston had inherited his playful nature from his father.

"Cheri thought you all were having a private moment."

"No, all our private moments are done in private," his father said teasingly and nuzzled his wife's neck.

"Yes, but we must curb our impulses now that PJ is here," she warned him.

"What, Cheri and I don't matter?" Preston asked and smiled at his parents.

"You and Cheri should understand. I'm sure spontaneity between the two of you is a norm in your castle."

"When PJ isn't there," Preston answered his father teasingly.

"Oh, let me up so I can stir my collards."

Bishop Owens tightened his hold. "Let your daughter-in-law do it, I want you right here."

Preston laughed at his father's playfulness. "See how openly affectionate they are?"

Cheri, now standing at the stove attending to the food, looked over to the refrigerator where her husband stood and said, "So what are you saying, I'm not affectionate?"

"You weren't last night," Preston said accusingly.

"Preston!" Cheri put her hand on her hip.

"What? We're married! They don't care what we do in our bedroom," Preston countered.

His father laughed out loud. "Oh, she gave you the old we can't, because it's your parents' house routine?"

"Oh, so you understand, then?"

"All too well, your mother used to do that to me when ever we'd visited your grandmother in Ohio."

"What did you do?" Preston asked.

"He rented a hotel room!" his mother answered.

Cheri laughed and so did Preston.

"Then I realized how silly that was, but only after my husband told my mother what we were doing," his mother explained.

Her father picked up the story. "Yes, my mother-in-law told my wife that the marriage bed is undefiled, so whatever we did in our sleeping quarters was our business and no one else. Read Hebrews 13:4."

"But I was only being considerate," Cheri protested. "I know how much noise Preston makes and I didn't want him to be embarrassed!"

Everyone laughed except Preston.

Chapter Eleven

Cheri had just completed her first full week of anchoring the morning news. She'd felt a little nervous in the beginning, but once she sat down to broadcast the words flowed out naturally, and the rating climbed each day, making the producers know that the audience connected with her performance.

"I must admit, Cheri, I thought it would take us some time before we would be able to gel together, but you've made a smooth transition—like only a true professional can." Her co-anchor extended his hand for a shake. "We make a wonderful team."

She ignored his hand and gave him a hug. "Thanks, Kevin. See you next week."

He nodded and walked away.

Cheri headed back to her office: she wanted to get home early today. She and Preston were headed to the Baptist Convention with the pastor and his wife. She'd only agreed to go because Preston truly wanted her to. What she really wanted was a leisurely weekend at home.

"Cheri, your son is on line seven," the receptionist informed her as soon as she reached the office wing.

"Thanks."

For the last few days, PJ had been calling her morning, noon, and night trying to get her to persuade his father to let him come back to Birmingham. So far, Preston was unyielding in his decision. After taking a deep breath she picked up the phone. "Hello, PJ."

"Did you talk to my dad?" He went right to the point of his call.

"Yes, and his answer is still the same."

"I don't want to stay here, I want to come home."

Cheri frowned. "PJ, what's going on?"

"Nothing, I just want to come home."

"You're with your mother, that's home, too. Why don't you want to stay with her?" There was dead silence on the phone. "PJ, are you still there?"

"Yes." He sounded like he was crying.

Cheri blew out a long sigh. "What's going on, sweetie? Why don't you want to stay with your mother?"

"I just want to be with my dad... and you."

There was a knock on the door. "Come in!" Cheri called. Tiffany rushed in with Amy in tow, "Hey, Cheri."

Cheri put her hand over the mouthpiece of the telephone and mouthed the words, "have a seat," while motioning to the guest chairs.

"Listen, your father and I will be at the Baptist Convention this weekend. I'll talk to him again while we're there, okay?"

"Okay. And, Cheri..."

"Yes."

"I'm sorry. Tell my dad I'm sorry too, okay."

"Okay. I have to go, but let's talk again on Sunday."

"I'll call you Sunday night."

"All right," Cheri said and hung up the receiver. "Tiffany, Amy, what's up? I'm really in a hurry, so..."

Amy planted herself near Cheri's closet door with her arms folded as Tiffany paced the floor hurling questions and answering them herself heatedly.

"She wanted me to have Ava. I didn't ask for her. Did I ask to become a mother? No. Did I need the aggravation of raising a child all by myself? Hell, no. Why is she doing this? Why?"

"What is going on?"

"She was just served with this." Amy flung a document on Cheri's desk.

Tiffany never stopped pacing. "I've known this woman all my life. I liked her better when she was a drunk."

Cheri looked up after gathering an understanding of what she had read. "Ava's grandmother has filed a partition to gain custody?"

"Yeah, and since she's the child's maternal grandmother, Tiffany thinks she'll win." Amy answered.

"Now I know why Brandon's been hanging around my house so much," Tiffany complained.

"Who is Brandon?" Cheri asked.

"Ava's uncle." Amy responded.

"Yeah, he's been setting me up for an ambush for his mother and all this because I'm not …. African American. Like her daughter didn't know that before she chose me to raise her child. Well, they can just go straight to hell, all of them. I don't need this, this… this crap."

"Tiff, calm down and have a seat. You can't think straight while being so enraged, I know I can't," Amy said.

"I don't have to think straight to know I love her," she yelled. "Love doesn't have color. Love is just love. What's so complicated about that?"

"You need a good attorney," Amy said.

"We've finally adjusted to each other, you know that, Cheri. You taught me how to do all those hairstyles she likes to wear. I took parenting classes and everything just to do right by my goddaughter. I invested to see this thing through and I can't just let them upset her world all over again. I won't have it and I'm not letting her go." Tiffany folded her arms in defiance.

"Hey, that's not going to happen and it's certainly not an option. You have the mother's wishes in writing," Cheri assured her.

"Her brother is on his way here now," Amy said.

"And he's an attorney," Tiffany added.

"What? Why?" Cheri asked. "I can't pretend here I understand everything that's going on right now, but…"

"Your husband on line three, Cheri," the clerk announced through her office private phone line.

"Give me a moment, ladies." She picked up the phone. "Hello … No, I'm on my way now. I was just about to leave." She looked over at Amy who had started out of her office with Tiffany. "See you within an hour." Cheri hung up the phone. "Tiff, if you need to talk…"

"I'll be fine. You try to enjoy the convention and don't let any of those religious fanatics tell you God isn't full of mercy and grace to forgive anyone for anything."

"Thanks. I'll remember that. And you call me if you need to talk. I'm leaving my cell phone on."

Tiffany gave her a thumbs-up gesture with a smile. "Enjoy yourself and I'll see you on Monday."

Cheri made it home in forty minutes. Preston had already loaded the luggage and was ready to go. By four that afternoon they were on Route 20 heading to Atlanta with Pastor Wright and his wife Bernice sitting in the rear seat of Cheri's late-model Mercedes.

By eight that evening the two couples had checked into their respective rooms at the Westin Hotel and were seated in the Sundial Restaurant, feeling totally in awe of the beautifully elegant decor. The tri-level dining complex located at the top level of the hotel was famous for the slowly rotating dining room allowing them a breathtaking 360-degree panorama of the magnificent Atlanta skyline.

"This place is stunning," Pastor Wright commented.

"It's gorgeous, sweetheart. I'm glad you finally agreed to come this year." Mrs. Wright beamed at her husband.

"Yeah, I'm glad I came too. I pray your room is to your satisfaction, Minister Owens."

"Oh, the room is perfect, pastor. Thank you."

"I hear they have those heavenly bed linens here. They tell me they're like sleeping on clouds."

"Well, I stayed here a few years ago, pastor, and believe me, I've never slept on anything remotely close to it."

"Then I can't wait to call it a night!"

Bernice cleared her throat. "Sister Owens, did you see all the wonderful sessions they have on women's auxiliaries?"

Cheri smiled, feeling Mrs. Wright was not at all comfortable with the men's conversation. "I took a quick glance, but since I'm a rookie at this I thought I'd let you take the lead and I'd just follow."

Mrs. Wright nodded. "Well, I think maybe we could go to the Layman's Wives & Women Supporters Prayer Breakfast at eight in the morning and then the exhibit hall or just go shopping right after that and have lunch on our own. Then maybe back to our rooms so we could get ready for the President's Educational Banquet at six with our husbands."

"Honey, Minister Owens may want to do some things with his wife, too."

"Oh, minister forgive me, I thought maybe you men wanted to hang out together while the women had some time to…"

"Shop," Pastor Wright supplied.

"Well, you hate to shop and I just thought maybe Cheri and I could go to the mall. I saw a flea market on our way in."

Pastor Wright dropped his head. "Well, we'll talk about the agenda tomorrow morning during breakfast." Then he directed his attention to Preston. "How does that sound, minister?"

"Sounds good, pastor," Preston said, glad the pastor had pulled the reins on his wife.

"Hello, Reverend Owens." Preston turned to see Pastor James Jones from Camden, New Jersey, who was a past moderator of the Bethany Association. Pastor Jones had been one of the men who had voted for him to resign as pastor.

"Pastor Jones, how are you?" he greeted the man with a forced smile.

"I'm doing just fine," Pastor Jones extended his hand for a shake.

"Reverend," Preston stood and greeted his wife, Patricia Jones, who ignored his hand and gave him a hug.

Preston placed a kiss on her cheek. "Mrs. Jones."

Cheri immediate felt uncomfortable. If anyone had shaken her to the root it would have to be these two people. He was senior pastor of the Cathedral of Faith Christian Center. He held a lot of power in the church community and was highly revered. His assistant pastor—who just happened to be his niece—was Miranda Jones. Miranda and Pastor Darrell Parker's wife Jade had been the best of friends since childhood. It was Pastor Jones' influence that aided in placing

Jade's husband, Darrell as pastor to the church that Preston had worked so hard to build. Reverend Miranda Jones never held her tongue when it came to bad-mouthing Cheri and Preston. She made it well known that she held no respect for either of them.

Cheri noticed Miranda coming up behind her aunt and uncle with a man before Preston did.

"Well, well. Hello, Reverend Owens, fancy meeting you here," Miranda said and smiled.

"Reverend," Preston's voice was aloof.

Pastor Wright cleared his throat loudly, making Preston remember his manners. "Forgive me. Pastor Cornel and Bernice Wright, Pastor James and Patricia Jones, and this is Reverend Miranda Jones."

Miranda held out her hand in greeting. "I'm Minister Waters now, I got married since Reverend Owens has been away. This is my husband, Kyle Waters." She made the announcement with pride, identifying the man who was standing just behind her.

"Pleased to meet all of you."

Pastor Wright and his wife greeted him while Cheri remained silent.

"Well, we'll go to our table. Enjoy your evening," Pastor Jones said. Then the group followed him as if he was pure royalty.

Preston blew out a long sigh.

"You're going to be fine, Son. Don't worry about them." Pastor Wright assured him.

"I really hate being around people I know don't like me. It makes me nervous … and Miranda hates me with a passion," Cheri said, taking a quick glance over at the table where they were sitting.

"She can't be much of a minister if she holds hatred in her heart," Mrs. Wright commented.

"Let's just pray that now that everything has come out in the open that everyone can forgive and forget. There are no perfect people, and that includes Minister Waters," was Pastor Wright's response.

ಬಂಗ

"Good morning, ladies." Cheri looked up to find Miranda Waters and Patricia Jones pulling out chairs to sit at their table. "I hope you don't mind us sitting with you." Patricia smiled then placed her plate on the table.

"There's a lot of people here," Miranda chimed in.

"Much more than last year," Patricia sat next to her niece.

"Good morning," Mrs. Wright greeted them with a smile.

Cheri felt like the wind had been sucked out of her lungs. She closed her eye to say a silent prayer to mind her manners.

"I hope the food's as good as it looks," Miranda folded her hands and quickly blessed her food.

"Are you sure God heard that prayer?" Mrs. Jones asked her niece.

"I'm starved. God doesn't need a long drawn-out prayer to bless my food." She placed a forkful of potatoes in her mouth.

Mrs. Jones glanced over at Cheri and Mrs. Wright. "She just found out she's pregnant. I noticed her appetite picked up way before she did."

"Congratulations," Cheri mumbled before focusing her attention back on her plate as jealousy crept to the surface. She didn't have much of an appetite in the first place, now the little hunger she had was completely gone.

"Is this your first?" Mrs. Wright asked Miranda.

"Yes, and I'm so excited!" She smiled widely.

Cheri dropped her fork into her plate and stood. "Excuse me," she said and quickly weaved her way past a few tables, past the buffet and out of the dining area. The women watched in complete silence as she made her exit.

Mrs. Jones finally spoke. "I don't think she was too happy about us joining you all for breakfast."

"Well, it's my understanding she's experienced a lot of church hurt from the people in your association. I assume she simply wants to avoid more of the same," Mrs. Wright pointed out.

Both Miranda and Mrs. Jones watched Mrs. Wright stand. "Please excuse me, ladies. I really think I should go after her."

"Certainly," Mrs. Jones answered.

Miranda nodded.

Mrs. Wright caught up with Cheri near the elevator doors just before she stepped on. "Where are you going?" she asked as soon as she approached her.

"To my room. I'm not feeling very well."

"Don't let the devil steal your joy," Mrs. Wright admonished her. "You do know the joy of the Lord is your strength?"

"You don't understand."

"I understand more than you think I do."

How could she know about wanting a child and feeling envious about another woman's joy of conceiving one, Cheri thought as she shook her head.

Mrs. Wright grasped her hand. "Come with me. Let's sit. I want to share my story with you."

Cheri followed Mrs. Wright to the lobby where they found a sofa near a picture window.

"Where can I start?" Mrs. Wright asked herself looking Cheri directly in the eyes. "Well, let me start near the beginning." She paused a moment, "I'm not the first Mrs. Wright. I'm actually the second first lady."

Cheri straightened her back and looked at Mrs. Wright with total surprise.

"I knew the first Mrs. Wright personally. She was a wonderful woman. Everyone loved and respected her for her grace and virtue. I aspired to be like her. She was ten years older than me and I looked up to her. When I turned eighteen she took me under her wing and trained me as her and pastor's secretary. Three years later, I became the church administrator. Everywhere she went, she took me with her. She was a preacher, too, you know. She was good at bringing the Word down to a level where just an average person could understand. I often told her she had the gift for communication."

She smiled, remembering. "Well, anyway, the whole church had been in a week revival at another church where the pastor had been the speaker. On that Saturday afternoon First Lady called me to say she wasn't feeling well and wouldn't be traveling with us. She assured me she would be fine. Well I stayed with her anyway, after all, I was not only the church administrator, I was her personal assistant too. Well anyway, the church left around six that evening and I called her at seven. She told me she was fine and fussed me out for not going with the church to the service. I called her again at eight and once again she told me she was fine. Then I called around nine and she told me to stop calling her cause she was trying to get some sleep."

"You were concerned," Cheri commented.

"Oh very much so, but I figured she was fine since she almost bit my head off for calling her so much. And since we were scheduled to have three services the next day, I went to bed. Pastor told me when he got home around eleven that night he went directly to their bedroom to check on her and she was gone, had died in her sleep."

"Oh, no, what caused her death?"

"She had a brain aneurysm."

"She had no symptoms?"

"Pastor said she complained about her neck being stiff earlier that day. But he just figured she was a little tried from going to the services every night that week."

"She never complained to you about a severe headache or anything?"

"No, but I assumed when I called her the last time she was trying to sleep because she had developed one. They found an opened bottle of Tylenol on her night stand."

"That had to be devastating for all of you."

"Oh, it was. It was unexpected and it happened so suddenly. She was my friend."

Cheri could tell the memory still affected her.

"I watched the pastor grieve for three years. During all that time he wouldn't even look at another woman. We talked about First Lady all the time during those first three years. What she would do in this situation or what she would have to say about that. Then one day, Penelope Payton stepped into the church and turned pastor upside down. He thought he was in love. Oh, she would cook for him and sing to him." She chuckled. "I can't lie, the woman could sing!" She paused a moment. "At first I thought she'd be good for him. She got him out of all that grieving he'd been doing. Then one day, he came into the office all excited and told me he was going to ask her to marry him. Then a week later he came into the office and told me that he decided not to ask her to marry him after all. I could tell he was upset so I didn't question him about it. I'd been working for him long enough to know that he'd come to me when he was ready to talk."

She sighed. "Everyone in the church figured I knew what had happened between the two of them and I kept telling them I didn't know a thing. I had no clue to what changed his mind about her. About a week later the pastor came into my office and just started talking about how he found out she was a liar and a cheat, too. He said she had a husband alive and well in Chicago and four pervious husbands to boot!"

"Wow!" Cheri was totally engulfed in her story.

"Then he burst out in tears. I felt so sorry for him and on instinct I wrapped that man in my arms and I let him cry."

"He needed that."

"The cry did him good and when he finished I told him that God would send him a Godly woman and to just be ready for when she comes."

"You still didn't know it was you?"

"No, child, I was dating Richard Adams at the time and we were gettin' serious, so I just knew he was gonna to be my husband."

"How old were you then?" Cheri was curious.

"I was twenty-four years old and ready to leave Birmingham to see the world. Richard was in the air force," she said matter-of-factly.

Cheri bobbed her head up and down. "Ooh, I see."

"Well, anyway, I noticed a change in the pastor after him and Penelope broke up. He became distant with me. I didn't know what I did or if I said anything to offend him, so after about three months of him treating me like I had the bubonic plague, I gave him my two week's notice.

"You resigned?"

"Had to. One week before, Richard married some woman from the Philippines."

"What?"

"Yes, he did. Wrote me one of those Dear Joan letters, and told me it was over. My feelings were hurt. I'd told everyone that any day now he was going to ask to marry me and that I'd be moving overseas. So, since I was so embarrassed, I'd made plans to move to Ohio with my cousin to start me a new life. She had been begging me to stay with her and so I decided to take her up on it."

"So after you gave him the notice, what happened?"

"He read the thing right in front of me, balled it up and tossed it in the wastebasket next to his desk."

Cheri gasped. "What?"

"Then had the nerve to order me to go back to my desk and for the rest of the day he acted as if I never even gave him my resignation."

"Wow."

"He came to my house that evening and told me he needed to talk to me. I knew he didn't want me to leave because I was good at my job, but I was ready to tell him off in a nice way and let him know I needed to leave for me. I needed to leave Birmingham and just go to a place away from him and the church. I needed to get a life. But I wasn't ready to hear him say, 'I love you, Bernice.'"

Cheri smiled, seeing the gleam in Mrs. Wright's eyes.

"It wasn't even the words that touched me so. It was how he said it. He told me he knew for a long time that he loved me, but didn't think it was right. So after Penelope came he tried to direct his attention and affection on her. I was forced to admit to him that I was going to marry Richard because I just knew the way I was starting to feel about him was inappropriate."

"Oh, so you were secretly in love with him?"

"No, not at all, I know for a fact I didn't feel that way about him while the first lady was alive. It developed over time long after she passed away, I'm sure of that."

"So you all declared your love for each other and now live happily ever after."

"Oh heavens, no, the church went crazy when the pastor called a meeting and told them that we would be dating."

"You're kidding."

"They said stuff like we'd been seeing each other for years and that I betrayed the first lady's trust. They said so many ugly things that I promised God I'd never repeat it. They acted like the first lady had just died yesterday and that I'd been carrying on an affair with the pastor for years."

"That had to be hurtful!"

"It was, and I'm telling you this because nobody knows church hurt like I know church hurt. When they talked about me so, I really did want to go to Ohio and start me a new life. Pastor wouldn't allow me to do that. He had a second church meeting and told them the truth and said if they didn't believe it that was their business and to take it up with God."

"Did it stop them?"

"Hardly! Church membership went down and the church struggled for a while. But the deacons stood by us and that made all the difference in the world. Now here we are some thirty years later and some of them same people that talked about me so bad is now gone and we're still here."

"You've been married for thirty years?"

"Thirty-two years. We raised two boys and two girls and we have six grandchildren now."

Cheri raised both eyebrows, "Pastor and his first wife never had children?"

Mrs. Wright smiled. "Our oldest, Naomi, she's their child. But I never separate her from the others."

"I've meet your youngest son Michael when he preached at the church a few months ago."

Mrs. Wright nodded. "The only one to follow in his father's footsteps."

"And I met Sarah, she came with Michael."

"Her and Michael attend the same church up in Chicago. One day soon you'll get to meet Cornel Jr. and Naomi. I wanted to tell you all this so you can understand that I know what you're going through. But if God be for you, it's more than the whole world against you. And I believe God is for you, Cheri. So don't let those women see you sweat. You hold your head up and show them that you are Mrs. Preston Owens and there ain't nothing they can do about it, all right?"

Cheri nodded and smiled. "All right."

Mrs. Wright stood up. "Now let's try and find someone to point us to the mall. I need a new hat."

Without warning Cheri stood, wrapped her arms around Mrs. Wright and gave her a kiss on her cheek. "Thank you."

She hugged her back. "Aw, you're welcome, sweetie."

After a full day of seminar sessions, a little shopping, and finally attending the worship service, both Preston and Cheri were exhausted.

"I felt like I was validated today," Cheri announced as she lay in her husband's arms.

"Validated, how so?"

"First Lady told me she's actually the second first lady. She said she was friends with the pastor's first wife."

Preston gasped. "She's his second wife?"

Cheri lifted her head from her husband's chest. "Can you believe that?" Cheri repeated the story Mrs. Wright had told her earlier that day.

"Well, they certainly love each other, there's no doubt about that."

"It's pretty evident," she agreed. "The pastor is almost thirteen years older than Bernice."

"We're on a first-name basis now?"

"I like her, Preston, and she likes me. So, yes, we're on a first-name basis."

"So how old is.... Bernice?"

"She's fifty-six."

"She looks good for her age."

"She does, and so does the pastor."

"Now I understand what he's preparing the church for."

"What's that?"

"Well since he's sixty-eight or maybe even sixty-nine, he knows retirement is approaching so he's trying to position the church for a smooth transition from one leadership to another."

Cheri raised her head to look into her husband's eyes. "Bernice said he's chosen you to succeed him. She said he keeps telling her that he's tired and want to relax and enjoy life a little."

"It never occurred to me he was looking for a successor, especially since he looks so much younger than he is."

She nodded in agreement. "He could pass for a man in his mid-fifties."

"Wonder why his son isn't the one taking over the church?"

"Bernice told me Michael is the assistant pastor of a mega church in the Chicago area and is being groomed there for that purpose, and she said he has no desire of returning to the south."

For a long while the couple snuggled in bed in complete silence. Cheri stroked her husband's chest, contemplating how to bring up the next subject she needed to discuss. Just when he was about to fall to sleep she whispered his name. "Preston."

"Hum." He tightened his hold on her.

"I want to bring PJ home."

There was silence.

"Preston, did you hear me?"

"Yes, and my answer is still no."

"Why?"

"He had his chance to live with us and he ruined it."

"He told me he was sorry. He asked me to tell you too." Preston was silent. "Please, give him another chance, I'm begging you."

"If I hadn't come home early that day, I wouldn't have known how nasty that boy could be. And you were ready to leave me."

"That wouldn't have happened."

"I heard you, Cheri." He was astonished that she would continue to deny her intent. "I heard what you said to him. You were hurt and the boy did it intentionally. Now you're campaigning for him to come back."

Cheri straddled her husband and ran her fingers through his hair. "He knows he was wrong and he's sorry. If I can forgive him, so can you."

Preston took in a deep breath and steadied his wife by holding her waist. "Baby, no." he said.

"Please do this for me. I need him to believe I persuaded you to bring him home. I want him to think I did this just for him." She leaned in closer, caressed his nose with her own, and kissed him lovingly.

Just when he felt himself enjoying it, he tore his lips away, "You are so wrong. You know you're wrong don't you?"

"Remove your hands from my waist," she whispered.

"No. I will not tell you the source of my strength, Delilah."

Cheri gave him a wicked smile. She liked playing this role with him. "But I love you, Samson." He released her and she threaded his fingers with her own.

He groaned. "You don't play fair."

"All is fair in love."

Chapter Twelve

"Knock, knock."

Cheri lifted her head from the computer screen to see Tiffany standing at her door. "Hey, come on in and have a seat. How was your weekend?"

Tiffany sat on the sofa and put her coffee mug on the end table next to her. "Interesting, how was yours?"

"You first," Cheri answered as she came to sit next to her. "I'm dying to know if you've straightened everything out with your goddaughter's family."

Tiffany smiled and said, "I have the support of her uncle."

"Well, that's a good thing, right?"

Tiffany nodded. "Maybe."

Cheri looked at her sharply. "I would think you'd be happy. Friday you thought he had an ulterior motive!"

"Well, let's just say I'm more optimistic," Tiffany said. "I'm just not celebrating until the final verdict is in."

Cheri looked at her suspiciously. "You're not telling me everything, are you?"

Tiffany paused, then said, "He says he's in love with me."

Cheri's eyes widened in surprise. "You're joking."

Tiffany shook her head. "He said he wants to get everything with Ava cleared up before discussing it further."

Cheri's left brow raised. "Ava's uncle..." She paused a moment as if to get her bearings, then started again. "Your best friend's brother... told you... he's... in love with you?" The words finally came out, loaded with surprise.

Tiffany stared at her and nodded slowly.

Cheri leaned forward in her chair. "And you didn't have a clue?"

"I knew he had an adolescent schoolboy crush on me when he was a child, but nothing like he explained to me on Saturday."

Cheri pressed her back against the chair. "Evidently the crush turned into much more."

Tiffany took a careful sip of her coffee, then nodded. "I've known him all his life. I was at his house with his sister when his parents brought him home from the hospital. I've always treated him like a little brother. His sister and I taught him how to walk, for goodness' sake!"

Cheri grinned. "Well, you're not his sister, and how much older are you anyway?"

"Almost six years."

"Well, neither of you are children anymore. Get beyond the legal matters, then deal with him."

Tiffany smiled. "Now you sound like him!"

"I think that's confirmation of good advice."

Tiffany nodded. "Enough about me. So how did the conference go?"

"It was good. I actually enjoyed being with the pastor's wife."

"See, you were worried for nothing thinking you were going to be bored!"

"I was wrong," Cheri agreed. Then she repeated the whole conversation she had with the pastor's wife about her being the second first lady.

"She really wanted you to know she could relate to your feelings," Tiffany said and beamed. "I like her, and I haven't even met the woman!"

Cheri smiled in agreement. "And I had a little chat with Reverend Miranda Jones, too."

"Who is she?"

"She's the minister that badmouthed Preston and me to everyone that would listen."

"Oh! I remember you telling me about her. Now that's one I don't like."

"Well, she apologized to us."

"Oh, did she?" Tiffany's voice was surprised.

"Just as we were loading the car to check out of the hotel she stopped Preston in the lobby. I saw them talking and I didn't want any part of the conversation, so I got in the car and waited for everyone so we could leave. When I saw Preston coming toward the car with Miranda I wanted to choke him."

Tiffany laughed. "So you were just a tad agitated?"

"Oh, just a little bit," Cheri agreed.

Tiffany shifted into a more comfortable position. "So tell me the whole story and don't leave out a thing."

"Preston opened the car door and asked me to step out for a minute."

With aid from her husband, Cheri grudgingly did as he asked and found herself standing face to face with Miranda. The expression on Cheri's face showed the animosity she felt toward the woman.

Miranda was a little fidgety when she spoke. "I just apologized to your husband for some of the things I've said to him, and about him, in the past. I spoke without knowing the facts and I was wrong to judge either of you. I want you to know that I was wrong and I'm sorry." Miranda held out her hand for a shake. "I hope you can forgive me."

Cheri stared at the hand being offered.

"I told Miranda you weren't petty." Preston revealed as Miranda continued to hold out her hand. "I hope you don't make a liar out of me."

Cheri looked directly at Miranda. "Things aren't always what they appear to be," then she took the hand offered for a shake.

"I know, and I've been properly chastised, believe me. Jade gave me a good tongue lashing."

"I'd forgotten you two are friends." Cheri said almost in a whisper.

"She's like a sister to me."

Cheri nodded, remembering that Jade had told her just that. Miranda and her cousin Ivy were the granddaughters of the founding pastor of Cathedral of Faith Christian Center where Ivy's father, Bishop James Jones, was pastor.

"Well, you all have a safe trip back, and I hope since we both have a friend in Jade that we can become friends as well."

Cheri was nonchalant. "Anything's possible."

Miranda smiled. "All things are possible," she agreed he before turning and walking away.

Cheri and Preston watched over the roof of the car as she headed back into the hotel. Pastor and Mrs. Wright exited the same set of doors Miranda had approached and they paused to chat.

"She had to swallow her pride to come to us and ask for forgiveness, and you were ice cold, baby," Preston criticized his wife.

"I wasn't cold, I was protective," she spat, defensively, before getting into the car.

Tiffany's outburst of laughter ended Cheri's recount of her meeting with Miranda. "I know you, Cheri. You can be coldhearted when you want to be."

"Enough about that! The best news of all is my stepson is coming home." Cheri said on a more happy note.

"You got your husband to change his mind!" Tiffany was thrilled. "Now I hope when he gets back he'll appreciate what you've done for him."

"Even if he doesn't, I won't stop trying to reach the gentle side of him. Anyway, he's not coming back until the school year ends, so his father and I will enjoy our solitude while we still have it."

"Oh, speaking of fathers, yours called while you were broadcasting. He wants you to ring him back. I'm out of here." Tiffany rose from the sofa. "I'm having a late lunch with Brandon."

Cheri was already at her desk punching in her father's number. "Make sure Brandon's not having you for lunch, cougar."

Tiffany was laughing as she made her exit.

"Hi, Daddy." Cheri was always glad to talk with her father. After having no communication for so many years it seemed they were trying to make up for lost time.

"Ma chérie amour, I called to see if I could come visit you. I need to get out of Philly."

"You are always welcome, Daddy. When are you planning to come here?"

"I was looking at the fourth. I'd like to come soon after my pension hits the bank."

"Daddy, you don't need money to visit me! Once you get here your money is no good anyway."

"Well, I'd like to have spending money to get the grandbabies something."

"Grandbabies, meaning more than one?" Cheri inquired.

"You know I have more than one. I want to get more acquainted with Sandra's children too. Nothing breaks the ice better than gifts."

"I thought you told me Sandra didn't want to speak with you."

"She still mule-headed all right, but I called the house and your mother let me talk with my grands."

"Oh, really." Cheri was surprised to hear that. "So you and Mama are on speaking terms?"

"Yup."

"How'd this come about?" Cheri was curious.

"She called me to tell me about this gala she's putting together for you and your husband. She told me she wanted me to be there."

"Oh, that's right. She did tell me she was going to invite you. I'd forgotten I gave her your number. Well, I'm glad you-all are talking. I hope Mama's behaving herself."

"We'll the first time we talked it was kinda rough. But by the end of the conversation she cooled off enough to order me to be in Alabama for your event."

Cheri laughed. "She hasn't changed one bit, Daddy."

"I know. I really didn't expect her to."

She smiled, even though she knew he couldn't see her. "What time is your flight?"

"I'm not taking the plane, I'm coming by train."

"Train! Daddy, that's going to be a long ride."

He chuckled. "I hate planes, and I just want to sit and relax in one of those rooms they have."

"Oh, so you're not riding coach?"

"Nope, those rooms have a bed and in the day they fold them up into a sofa. I'm gonna sip some wine and watch the scenery from my private window. The train leaves 30th Street Station at three fifty-five in the afternoon and it get to Birmingham the next morning at eleven forty-five. I know you and your husband will be at work so I'll just take a taxi to your house."

"I can get someone to pick you up."

"No, I'll get a taxi. I'll probably drop my bags off at your house then go straight to the Birmingham Civil Rights Institute."

"I'll go with you, if you wait until I get home from work. I've lived here all this time and I've never been there."

"There'll be other opportunities for us to sightsee, baby girl, 'cause I want to visit a lot of places while I'm there. There's the Alabama Jazz Hall of Fame and the Sixth Street Baptist Church and ..."

Cheri laughter halted his list. "I get it, Daddy. So how long are you staying?"

"A whole week and that should give me enough time to see everything I want."

"I'm sure it will. Just save a little time to spend with me, all right?"

"I'll be doin' my sightseeing while you're at work. So don't worry, we'll spend time together. And by the way, since your mother has decided your reception is going to be there in Birmingham, she told me 'bout some place she saw on the internet called, hold on, I have it written down ... The Hill Event Center, it's adjacent to the Alabama Theatre. She said it has two rooms, the banquet hall and the loft and she wants me to take pictures and check it out."

"I've never been there, however I sure it's nice, but..."

"Hold on, I'm reading what she gave me off this paper. The banquet hall is highlighted by 85-year-old chandeliers from the grand ballroom of the original

Tutwiler Hotel in Birmingham. The loft overlooks the Alabama Theatre marquee and 3rd Avenue. The Hill Event Center provides a setting unlike any other. It hosts such events as wedding receptions, corporate events, holiday parties, and formals."

"But I thought Mom wanted the whole family to come. Having it here would be an inconvenience for everyone. It would be so much easier if Preston and I come there."

"You'll have to take that up with your mother. I'm simply checking the place out for her."

"Okay, I'll get with her."

"Good."

Cheri and her father talked a little more and after she hung up the phone she rubbed her hand over her belly. She had felt a little sluggish for the last few days. She knew any minute now her menstruation would make its appearance. When she got home she went straight to her room, crawled into bed, pulled her legs up in a fetal position and drifted off to sleep.

That's where Preston found her when he came home a few hours later. Her eyes popped opened when he sat on the bed. Without saying a word he began to gently rub her back. She stared at him and he smiled. The only reason why she would be lying down this time as day was clear. "You're not feeling well?" He kissed the tip of her nose. He was concerned.

She shook her head. "No."

"Want me to get you anything?"

"I've already taken some Advil."

"Have you eaten?"

"I don't want food."

"Did you eat anything today?"

"I had some juice," she admitted.

Preston's hand came to a standstill. "It's six in the evening, sweetheart, and all you've had is juice today?"

Cheri sat up. "I just haven't had an appetite."

"You promised me you'd do better. You won't be able to gain a pound at this rate," he said sharply.

Cheri relaxed her head against the pillow. "I'm sorry. I really want my appetite to pick up."

"Well, I guest the appointment with your gynecologist has to be cancelled."

Cheri raised her head from the pillow. "Why would I want to do that?"

Preston stared at her a moment more, then stood. "I'm sure she can't examine you properly…"

"That appointment is next week," she snapped cutting him off.

"No, it's not. I took off the whole morning to go with you. I know that appointment is tomorrow unless you changed the date and didn't inform me."

"Are you sure?" She was perplexed.

"I'm pretty sure."

Cheri sprang from the bed to look at her appointment on her digital calendar. She searched through and noticed first her husband was right. The appointment for the specialist was tomorrow and her menstruation was more than a week late. "How could I have made this mistake?"

"You need to eat, your brain isn't registering to the top because it needs fuel, sweetheart."

Cheri smiled. "I scheduled this appointment so it would be after my monthly. This means I'm more than a week late. I've felt sluggish, but it never made an appearance."

Preston came to stand next to his wife. "So does this mean you just may be with child?"

"It's possible," Cheri said calmly but on the inside she was overjoyed.

ೲ಄ಐ

The next day, Preston accompanied his wife to the medical facilities and after she was examined thoroughly they sat in the visitors' chairs and watched as the doctor flipped through pages in her file waiting to hear the verdict.

"From the test we've taken today there is no indication that you're pregnant," the doctor said gently, knowing that wasn't the news this couple wanted to hear.

Cheri couldn't believe her ears. "But I'm never late, never."

"You've lost a lot of weight since the last time I saw you and as a matter of fact you're underweight, which is probably why you haven't menstruated."

Preston raised his head. "I don't understand."

"Well, your body has to have fat in order to menstruate and it seems that your wife has lost too much fat. Body weight should be within five percent of normal body weight for her menstrual cycle to "behave" normally. If your body fat percent is too low, you won't get your period. When you don't have enough nourishment, your body will stop supporting your reproductive cycle and focus on the basic necessities like eating, breathing, thinking, because there isn't enough energy to support every body function." Then she looked directly at Cheri. "So if you really want to get pregnant you'll have to get your weight up."

Cheri wanted to cry, and it took everything within her not to drop a tear.

"Medically did you see anything that's stopping her from gaining weight or anything that's suppressing her appetite?" Preston asked, truly concerned about his wife's health.

"Well, she has chronic anemia and I'm going to prescribe 50,000 milligrams of vitamin D." She picked up her pad and started writing. "You'll take that only once a week. I'm also putting you on vitamin C and iron and you'll take that daily. I want to see you in four weeks. At that time I'll take some blood and see how you're progressing. I want you to be no less than three pounds heavier."

When Cheri didn't answer, Preston grasped his wife's hand. "We're going to do just that, doctor."

"Good." She smiled at Preston before turning back to his wife. "Cheri, you're going to be fine. My nurse is printing a special list of foods for you to add to your diet. I promise, if you give your body what it needs, you'll get what you want from it, okay?"

"Okay," Cheri answered weakly.

Chapter Thirteen

Cheri had been in a depressed mood in the days leading up to her father's visit. Nevertheless, she made a conscious effort to eat and to do her job with expertise, and the ratings continued to climb. Now it was Friday and her father had arrived a few hours ago and was already at her house. He had taken a taxi from the train station and used the key she placed under the welcome mat. She was excited about spending quality time with him.

Cheri had taken the time to redecorate the spare bedroom just for his comfort. She'd purchased a 42-inch flat screen television and had the satellite extended to that room. She wanted his stay to be pleasant and memorable.

When she stepped through her front door, the delicious aroma of the food lead her directly toward the kitchen. "Daddy!" she squealed as he approached her with his arms stretched wide for an embrace.

"Ma chérie amour!" He hugged her tightly. "I have a surprise for you," he whispered near her ear.

When he released her she saw her mother's smiling face. Her eyes widened with surprise, "Mama!" She rushed to her, giving her a tight hug as well and after kissing her cheek, she exhaled, "I didn't know you were coming."

"I know, I told your father not to tell you."

"Well, he certainly knows how to keep a secret!"

"Don't get comfortable. I need to get some things from the store. You don't have a leaf of sage in your cabinets."

"Since PJ isn't here I haven't been doing a lot of cooking."

"Well, from the weight you've lost since I last saw you, I can see that," her mother said after appraising her. "So while I'm here I'm going to fatten you and Preston up."

Cheri stared at her mother. She looked different. "You colored your hair."

"I took the gray out. Do you like it?"

"You look wonderful."

"She looks better than wonderful,' her father beamed with admiration as he ogled her mother.

Then Cheri realized there were sparks firing between them. "What's going on?" she asked suspiciously, since her mother was smiling at her father as he looked at her as if she had dazzled him. "Mama, what…"

Bernadette interrupted, ignoring her daughter. "We need to get to the store so I can finish dinner." She stepped around Cheri's father to grab her purse. "The cornbread is in the oven, so don't let it burn while we're gone. Let's go, Cheri," she ordered as she made her way to the front door.

Cheri followed her mother out to the car. After settling on the passenger side, Bernadette pulled out a list of groceries. "The store isn't too far, is it?"

"No," Cheri answered as she pulled out of the driveway onto the road.

"Good. Now, I want to get some cube steaks for dinner tomorrow, so don't let me forget. I forgot to put it on this list. Your father's always loved my steak and gravy."

Cheri halted for the traffic light and looked at her mother with curiosity. "Mama, what's going on between you and Daddy?"

"What do you mean?"

"Please don't insult my intelligence."

"Since you're so intelligent, it should be obvious what's going on." Her mother gave Cheri a wicked smile.

Cheri stared at her mother until a car horn honked behind her. She stepped on the gas. "You and Daddy are having an affair?"

"Don't be silly. How am I going to have an affair with my own husband?"

Cheri's bottom jaw dropped and thirty seconds later another car horn snapped her out of her shocked expression.

Cheri made a left turn and merged into traffic. "It's hard for me to wrap my mind around the thought of you two being together again after so many years apart."

Cheri was overwhelmed by the revelation of her parent's obvious reconciliation. She quickly turned the wheel to avoid hitting a car.

Her mother clenched her chest and said, "We're not going to discuss this anymore until we get back to your house. Now, I want to see Jesus, but I'm not in no hurry. So keep your eyes on the road and pay attention."

Later that evening, Preston was shocked to find out his inlaws had traveled together by train. From what he and his wife had witnessed as the two worked beside each other in the kitchen preparing dinner, the truce between Bernadette and Jeffery had not just started. That was evident just from watching the interaction between them. Especially after Bernadette spooned a sample of the rice and beans into Jeffery's mouth for him to taste.

"Oh this is good, sweetness." Jeffery closed his eyes and chewed slowly.

"It doesn't need more salt?" Bernadette asked.

"No, it just needs to go onto my plate to be eaten."

Bernadette was still beaming with pride at his remark when she glanced over at her daughter who was totally mystified by the exchange. Bernadette quickly composed herself by blinking her eyes and taking a deep breath. "Have you set the table, Cheri?"

Cheri nodded still struggling with what her eyes had seen and ears have heard. "Preston is already sitting, waiting for the food," she stammered.

Once the food was placed on the table and the blessing had been said, Preston asked the question he'd wanted to ask since he got home. "How did this treaty between you two come about?"

Jeffery spoke with measured timing. "We both decided to let the past stay in the past. I've always loved her and she's never stopped loving me. So it seemed pretty crazy to allow our past mistakes to dictate our tomorrow."

"Did you-all decide this after talking on the phone that first time?" Cheri asked, looking for an answer from either one of her parents.

It was her mother who answered. "No, we met at our favorite restaurant a few times, and that's all you need to know," with finality.

Cheri's mouth was agape. Preston picked up the conversation. "Well, let me just say that I'm glad to see the peace between the two of you. However, we do have a problem."

"Which is?" Bernadette asked.

"My wife only prepared the one room and…"

"Bernie can sleep in the room you arranged for me," her father offered. "I can sleep anywhere. The couch will be fine,"

"No, Daddy, you don't have to sleep on the couch. Preston's son's room is available, but it has bunk beds."

"I can sleep on a bunk bed," he assured her with a smile.

"No, that wouldn't be fair, the room was set up for your stay so…"

"Why can't you both sleep in there?" Preston asked. "It's a king-sized bed, and…"

"Preston!" Cheri gasped.

"What? They're still married and just because they're sleeping in the same room doesn't mean…"

"I was about to suggest just that," Bernadette agreed.

"What?" Okay, just a month ago her mother didn't want her to say her father's name in her presence, and now they were able to share a room?

"We slept in the same room on the train, so what's the difference?" Bernadette reasoned.

"Then it's settled. We'll share the room," Cheri's father announced as if it were the most natural thing to do.

By the third day of her parents' arrival it was obvious the trip had not been planned to spend time with her, and Cheri felt two emotions at the same time. Jealousy, because she had not been included in their daily adventures of touring the city, and joy because this was the first time her mother's laughter was so genuine. She was relaxed and enjoying life and that was enough to overlook any feelings of abandonment.

On the evening before Cheri's parents' departure, Preston set up the grill to barbeque baby back ribs using his secret recipe sauce, and Cheri prepared her famous deviled eggs and baked beans.

"You know this is the first time we had to cook since your mother's been here," he said to his wife while turning the meat.

"It's been nice coming home to home cooked meals everyday this week."

"Everyone's enjoyed it except you," Preston said.

"Don't be silly, I've enjoyed them just as much as you have."

Preston shook his head at her comment. "I think you're suffering from anorexia, and your mother thinks so too."

"Now that's just silly." Cheri waved her hand at the accusation.

"Well you have many of the classic signs, sweetheart. Dramatic weight loss in a short period of time, obsession with calories in the food you eat, wearing baggy clothes, always complaining that the camera adds weight to your appearance."

"And just this morning I watched you add water to your orange juice," her mother said as both her parents approached them.

Preston grunted. "Need I say more?"

"So what are you saying? I'm not voluptuous enough for you? Cheri asked her husband a little harshly.

"This is not about the way you look, it's about your health."

"Listen to what they are saying, ma chérie amour," Jeffery said to his daughter after placing a bowl of potato salad on the picnic table.

"So what is this, some kind of intervention?" Cheri was getting upset.

"Don't be so defensive, we're really concerned about you." Bernadette said.

"Well, don't be. I'm fine, really."

"That's the problem, you're not fine. You heard what the doctor said and you're still cutting calories. Why?"

Cheri raised her head to answer her husband and noticed her parents were waiting on her answer too. "Habit."

Preston put down the spatula and came to where his wife was standing. "That's only another word for addiction, baby. Let's break this now before it gets too far, okay?" Preston pulled her close to him and whispered in her ear, "I thought you wanted to have a baby."

She closed her eyes and rested her head on his chest. "Badly."

"Eat, that's all it's going to take."

"I'll do better, I promise," she whispered.

"I'm going to help you keep that promise," he declared, giving her a tight squeeze.

Chapter Fourteen

April quickly turned into May, and May to June, and at the end of that month PJ arrived with a whole new attitude toward her. Cheri could not help making reference to that change when he entered her home office the first Saturday after his return.

"I cleaned my room," he announced proudly.

Cheri lifted her head from the computer screen and, giving him a wide smile, she looked past him. "Excuse me, young man, but have you seen my stepson?"

PJ looked at her in confusion.

"I was wondering if you'd seen him, because the person I know as my stepson would never have announced cleaning his room with so much pride, nor without an argument, so maybe you've seen him walking around here somewhere. He's about your height and weight and we call him PJ"

PJ laughed loudly. "Oh, that guy doesn't live here anymore."

"Really, what made him change his address?"

He dropped his shoulders. "My grandmother told me everything. She even told me my sister was my half sister."

Cheri's eyes widened in surprise. "Oh, sweetie, I'm so sorry your parents didn't get a chance to explain everything to you in their own way."

"What other way is there to say your mother is a slut, than to just say it?"

Cheri gasped. "P.J! I won't have you speak of your mother that way, not in front of me."

"You're protecting her?"

"It's not about that, young man, it's disrespectful to say that about the woman who brought you into this world."

PJ tilted his head to one side. "You're totally different than I thought you were. I'm really sorry for the stuff I said to you and the way I treated you. Now, that was disrespectful. Especially since no matter how I treated you, you were always nice to me."

Cheri dropped her gaze to the floor. "PJ, we all make mistakes. No matter who we are, we are all human and we make bad choices sometimes. God knows, I've made some pretty huge mistakes of my own. I'm still making them on occasion."

"Yeah, well, I understand now why you and my dad got together."

Cheri crossed her arms over her breast. "Oh, you do?"

"Yeah, my dad should've married you from the beginning."

"PJ, if your father had done that where would that have left you?"

He nodded. "It would leave you as my mother."

"No, it wouldn't."

"So what are you saying? My mom's husband could be my dad?"

"No, I'm not saying that at all. You could only be you the way you came to be you, through the genes of your mother and father. That alone was worth them getting married. Both of them love you beyond belief and wouldn't change you for all the tea in China."

PJ dropped his gaze to the floor. "My grandmother told me that my dad always loved you, so when my mom didn't want him anymore, the two of you got back together."

"I was wrong to get involved with your father the way I did. The best way to look at any matter would be to ask, what would Jesus do? I know God was not pleased the way we adults handled this whole thing."

"Well, my grandmother said she doesn't blame you and that my dad should have gotten rid of my mom years ago. She said my dad is a good man who tried to make the best out of a bad situation."

"Well, your grandmother may be just a little partial toward your father."

"Why you say that?"

"He's her son, PJ"

"Son-in-law." PJ corrected.

Cheri turned quickly. "Your mother's mother is the one who talked to you about this?"

"Yeah, she said I had a right to know."

Cheri was astounded. "And you haven't told your parents?"

"I finally told my mom this morning. She was sweating me about not calling her and letting her know how I was doing. So I told her I was mad at her and I really didn't have anything to say to her."

"You do know it's not right to disrespect your parents?"

"She gets no more respect from me, I'm done with her."

Cheri paused to get her thoughts together. "PJ, sit down for a moment and let me talk to you."

He complied without a single word.

"I know you're probably hurt by what your grandmother told you. I understand totally. I came from a broken home, too. My mother and father split up when I was younger than you. For years I thought it was my father who was the villain, but I found out that the blame was all the adults involved."

"If all the adults were wrong, that means you and my dad were wrong too?"

Cheri nodded. "We made mistakes," she said.

His brows came together. "What did you do wrong?"

Cheri took a deep breath and exhaled. "I allowed a relationship to develop between your father and me before he was divorced."

"But my mom didn't want him!"

"It didn't matter. I was wrong in the sight of man and God."

PJ stood up. "My grandmother said sometimes people are forced to do stuff they wouldn't ordinarily do." He pushed the chair back in place. "Do you want me to do anything else around the house?"

He had changed the subject smoothly. Cheri quickly decided not to press the issue. "Did you change your sheets?

"Yeah, I put the dirty ones in the laundry room."

"Then no, everything else is done."

PJ started to walk away then turned quickly. "Oh, did you eat?"

Cheri slowly turned in his direction. "Oh no, not you, too."

He smiled. "Dad said you forget to eat sometime and that we had to look after you."

"Oh, really?"

"Yeah, so did you?"

She nodded. "Yes, I did."

"What did you eat?"

Cheri squinted her eyes at him. "Are you serious?"

"Hey, I'm just taking orders and being obedient. Didn't we just talk about me being respectful?"

Cheri stood and began searching the room. She looked behind the desk, she moved the chair to look under the desk. She moved to the closet, opened the door to search there as well.

PJ postured with his hands. "What are you doin'?"

"I know for a fact that you are an imposter. You are not my stepson."

He broke out in uncontrollable laughter and Cheri soon followed. After PJ closed the door Cheri felt a gentle calm settle around her. PJ had finally opened up to her in a way she never thought possible. She knew now that they had indeed reached a truce.

She closed her eyes momentarily thanking God and appreciating the victory. Briefly forgetting about her own dilemma, she couldn't wait until Preston came home so she could share with him the conversation she'd with his son.

Preston got home a short time later with the food PJ had placed on order. They sat at the table as a family. Though Cheri's appetite still had not picked up, she forced herself to eat, if only because PJ had shown so much concern. Every time she sat to eat a meal it reminded her of her physical problems that underlined the depression threatening to consume her. So she tried thinking of the good things that were happening in her life. She and her half-brother were well on their way to building a relationship, her mother's illness was in remission, and most of all, her parents had reconciled.

Just thinking about her parents made her smile. Both of them were working together to pull off the reception of a lifetime, slated to take place on the third Saturday in October.

After they ate, Cheri cleared the table while the men moved to the basement. Preston and PJ had been working for the last two evening on building a home theater system. After she cleaned up she started to go downstairs to see how they were progressing. But when she heard them laughing and enjoying each other's company, she decided to let father and son have their time together, alone.

She made her way up to her bedroom with all intentions of taking a long soak in the tub, surrounded by candles and a Christian novel by one of her favorite authors. But no matter how much Cheri tried, her mind went back to her dilemma. It had been over two months since she'd seen the doctor, and had been doing everything he told her to do. She'd even gained five pounds, yet she still had not had a menstrual cycle. Once again she thought about using in vitro fertilization. She had to convince Preston to at the least try his own sperm.

It was half past nine and Preston was still in the basement with PJ Then Cheri did something she had not done in a very long time. She knelt at the side of the bed and prayed.

June quickly turned into July, and July into August, and September rolled in with strong winds and stormy weather. It was the first Sunday in the month and Cheri just did not feel like getting up and dressing to attend church service. Preston was already in the shower getting himself ready to be at the church for the eight o'clock service.

For the last few weeks Cheri just had not felt like attending church at all, and this morning she decided to give church a rest. She was tired of going there every week, smiling when she felt like crying. Going into the house of God and leaving the same way she came, unfulfilled, feeling more depressed than the week before. She had stopped praying, she stopped begging God for a child. It just did not feel right to beg Him over and over again, when He knew what she so desired.

"Good, you're awake. I thought I'd let you sleep until the last minute," Preston said, leaning over to kiss her.

"Go away. I haven't brushed my teeth," she complained.

"Like I haven't smelled your bad breath before! Come on, get up, I don't want to be late today."

"I'm not going to church. I don't feel well."

Preston stared at her for a moment. "Has your period started?"

She shook her head. "No."

"Then what's wrong?"

"I don't know. I just don't feel like going."

Preston sat on the side of the bed nest to her. "I've been watching you for the last few weeks and you've been acting strange."

"How so?"

"You're not as feisty as your usual self and you're moody, Even PJ has noticed it."

Cheri felt like she might as well tell him. "I've been fighting depression for months. I think it's getting the best of me. I think I need to seek professional help."

Preston noticed the water welling in the corners of her eyes. "Baby, you need to give everything to the Lord."

"I've done that. But faith without works is dead. I've been lying here contemplating my options. Adoption is fine with me, but you won't hear of it, and you're dead set against me being artificially inseminated, and I don't understand why when we could try your sperm first."

Cheri rolled onto her side, turning away from her husband.

Preston shook his head and reached for her.

"Leave me alone."

He attempted to pull her onto his lap and she struggled to stay free.

"I'm never leaving you alone as long as I have breath in my body." He had cradled her halfway on his lap.

She wanted to cry but when she looked at him she could tell he was concerned. "Why are you staring at me?"

"I like looking at you." He smiled, then kissed her on the forehead, then kissed her cheek, the tip of her nose and finally her eyes.

"What time is it?" Cheri asked stopping his kisses.

Preston looked over at the clock on the dresser. "Six forty-five."

Cheri closed her eyes tightly. Preston had told her over a month ago that he had no intentions of having another verbal fight about adoption and babies again. At that very moment, Cheri decided to do the same. "If you don't mind I'm going to have a lazy day."

"It's all right with me, but you're probably hungry since you didn't eat last night."

"No, I'm fine. I don't want food, Preston."

"It doesn't matter what you want it's what you need. So if you want we can go to iHop and get some blueberry pancakes. You love them."

Cheri raised her body in a sitting position, "I thought you had to preach this morning."

"I do, but I told the pastor some time ago that you hadn't been feeling well and I may have to stay home with you, so I'll call him and let him know this is one of those times."

Preston had known for weeks Cheri was falling into depression and that he was the reason for it, but he had to have enough faith for both of them. "You do realize you need to eat, especially since you're losing weight again?"

"I've gained thirty-three pounds in the last five months. I'm sure one pound lost is only water weight, Preston."

"Thirty-three pounds and you're still too small. This can't be healthy," he countered, pressing his finger against her collarbone.

She swatted at his hand. "I just saw the doctor a month ago, and you know as well as I do, that I'm more healthy than I've been in months." She moved from the bed toward the bathroom. "Spend some quality time with your son." She practically slammed the door between them.

"My son informed me last night that he's planning on having company over today and asked if I could order a few pizzas after church. So since he has plans, why can't I spend the day with you?"

"I told you I'm having a lazy day," she whined.

"Then I'm going to be lazy with you, all day," he countered.

The phone interrupted their sparring. Preston answered it on the second ring.

Cheri turned on the shower and adjusted the temperature. She wanted to be alone and wallow in her misery.

Preston knocked rapidly on the bathroom door and pushed it open. "That was the first lady, they're rushing the pastor to the hospital. I need to get to the church."

Chapter Fifteen

Preston and Cheri had dressed in record time and, with PJ in tow, they rushed to the church. Cheri forgot the pity party she had planned to have for herself that day; not being at her husband's side during his time of need was simply not an option.

When they arrived at the church, Deacon Roberts escorted them directly to a room adjacent to the fellowship hall to meet with the chairman of the deacon board and the chairman of the trustees. They were waiting by the phone to hear a word from anyone who had accompanied the pastor and first lady to the hospital.

Preston knew of only one thing to do when he glimpsed the faces of the worried men. "Come, let's join hands and pray." Cheri immediately grasped her husband's hand and all the other men in the room formed a circle.

The prayer that Preston rendered did not last long, however the words were decisive and everyone felt the air around them being charged with the power of the Holy Spirit. Even Cheri's wavering faith was stirred and moved to tears.

"He's going to be all right, baby." Preston pressed his wife against his chest. What he didn't know was that his wife's tears were for herself. While Preston was praying he asked God to "allow us to accept your will above our own, make us know that your will is what's best for us, no matter what our hearts desire."

Cheri wanted that for herself more than anything. She wanted to accept the things she could not change and have the wisdom to know when to give what she had no control over to the Lord, completely.

Not long after she totally surrendered her dilemma over to God, the phone rang and it was Deacon Jones with the news that the pastor had a stroke.

Preston preached both the eight and the eleven o'clock services. The atmosphere was charged with faith and prayers of the church family for the pastor to have a quick and speedy recovery.

Preston did not preach long and reminded the congregation of the power of prayer and to remain prayerful. "All things work together for the good to them that love the Lord." He said during both services. "For we know that our pastor loves the Lord and he is the called of the same God he loves. Now, let's watch as God performs a miracle. As soon as Preston gave the benediction, Cheri and PJ made their way to meet him in the pastor's study. Cheri had decided to go home with PJ and allow Preston to go to the hospital to be with the pastor's wife.

Preston found Cheri in the family room drowsily watching television when he came home later that evening. She watched him place a legal-sized package on the end table before sitting in the chair across from her. Cheri lifted her body into a sitting position, picked up the remote to the television and muted the sound. "You look tired. Are you hungry?"

"No, a few of us took the first lady to the hospital café. The food was really good."

"Well, I'm glad you ate."

Preston tilted his head and looked at her suspiciously. "Have you eaten?"

Cheri smiled. "Yes, PJ made sure of that."

Preston smiled back at her. "That's my boy. Have you lost any weight?"

"No."

"How do you know?"

"I weigh myself every few days. I have a scale in my office at work and here in our bathroom. I made you a promise and I'm keeping up with it."

Preston nodded. "Thank you, sweetheart."

"So what is the pastor's prognosis?"

"He's stable and all I can say is God is truly a good God. The emergency room doctors knew exactly what was happening and admitted him. He was just in time to have a CT scan of his head. So they were able to administer a clot-busting medication called tissue plasminogen activator. The doctors called it t-PA. From what I understand this medication works with the body's chemicals and helped to dissolve the blockage in the pastor's brain that more than likely caused the stroke."

"They were able to stop the stroke?" Cheri asked

"No, but they were able to stop what could have been the lost of his independence. The stroke team took the information the pastor and his wife gave them and determined that this drug could be administered within three hours of the onset of his symptoms, so his prognosis for a full recovery is excellent."

"The wonder of modern medicine is so amazing."

Preston leaned his head against the back of the chair. "Yes, it is."

"I know you didn't leave his wife there alone?"

"Of course not, I stayed until her oldest son came and when I was leaving their oldest daughter had reached there as well. Their two other children from Chicago will probably be there before the night is over.

They told Deacon Roberts they would be here as soon as they could get a flight out."

"I'm glad all her children are coming to be here with her."

"Yeah, being surrounded by family has to make a difficult situation seem easier."

Cheri yawned. "I'll call her from the station tomorrow and maybe even stop by the hospital before I come home."

"I'm sure she'll appreciate that, baby."

"You want me to run you a tub of water, or do you just want to rest?"

"I'll hit the shower. Where's PJ?"

He's down in the theater with a few of his friends watching that new 3-D movie you downloaded."

"I can't believe he's watching it without me."

Cheri giggled. "I'll watch it with you when you're ready. I'll even nuke some popcorn and make your favorite frozen cherry slush drink."

Preston smiled. "You have a deal."

Cheri picked up the remote from the coffee table and switched off the television.

He hesitated. "Deacon Roberts said that pastor knew something was going to happen to him. He said before he left for the hospital he gave him that." Preston pointed to the envelope he tossed on the end table when he came in.

"Well, what is it?"

"As far as I can tell it's information and instructions about his vision for the church."

"Well, you already knew he'd been positioning himself to pass the torch."

"I think he's a little premature. Nevertheless, since Deacon Roberts told me I'm to step in his place until he's recovered, I'll continue his plans until his return."

"Well, I'm sure you'll make him proud." Cheri rubbed the back of her neck and stood. "Now that you're home, I'm going to bed. I have Sean Franklin breathing down my back trying to take my place as anchor."

"I didn't know your job was in jeopardy?"

"I don't think it is, it's just that I haven't been feeling well and all my colleagues have noticed. Sean is young and ambitious just the type of person to stab me in the back for the position."

Preston nodded. "You're good at your job so don't concern yourself with … Sean."

Cheri stood with a wobble.

Preston reached for her. "You all right?"

"I'm fine, just tired. See that PJ gets to bed at a decent hour." She headed for the stairs. "Goodnight, Preston."

"Night, sweetheart."

It was not long before September whirled into October and in the middle of that month depression hit Cheri with such force that she made an appointment for a psychiatric evaluation without telling anyone. That appointment was scheduled for December.

She was sure she knew that the source of her mental problems was her reproductive system not kicking in even after following the doctor's orders to the letter. She felt she needed help to overcome her depressed state.

Up until the beginning of October she had gained a total of thirty-nine pounds since April. Now she was losing weight again more rapidly than she had before. When she stood on the digital scale in her office last Friday she could not believe the number she read.

Oh, no: five pounds. She had lost five pounds in one week. When she stood on the scale Wednesday, she had lost another three pounds. Now the scale showed a total of nine pounds in two weeks. When she started working on her weight in April she thought that she would feel better immediately after she began taking in enough calories, especially after her weight had picked up. But her appetite was no better than it had been before and her emotional state had not improved either.

It was Friday and Cheri had her appointment with a new doctor, and Tiffany had accompanied her. Tiffany suggested that she get a second opinion about her physical health and it was she who had made today's appointment, convincing Cheri that this woman was a great physician with an impeccable record and a personal friend of hers.

Cheri was tired and that was nothing new. She had complained that carrying all the extra weight was causing her fatigue. She had gone from a size four to a size eight and she knew that had to have had an effect on her.

Before today's appointment Cheri had not met this doctor, but she had already started evaluating her by ordering lab work on her blood and urine on last Monday.

"Will you stop shaking your leg, the exam is over and now maybe you can get some answers to your dilemma," Tiffany said, giving Cheri a sideways glance.

"I don't know why I let you talk me into this. Every doctor I see says the same thing. 'There's nothing wrong with you,'" she mimicked. "Just gain some weight." Cheri rolled her eyes.

"Kat is a young doctor but she's smart. She was always a bookworm and…"

"Tiffany had all the dates and I couldn't get any." Dr. Katherine Cook said as she stepped into her office.

"That's why you graduated top of your class in med school and I barely made it out of undergrad."

"I was your roommate in undergrad and you just didn't take the time to study to get better grades. On the other hand, that's all I did. I missed out on a lot as a result, too."

Tiffany waved her hand. "What's going on with my friend? I'm tired of seeing her suffer and I know you can help her."

Dr. Cook directed her attention back to Cheri. "Do you want to discuss your personal medical history in front of her? She pointed at Tiffany. "I will kick her out of the room right now. HIPAA law," She turned to Tiffany. "Sorry."

"No, I understand." Tiffany attempted to stand.

"No, I want you to stay." Cheri grasped Tiffany's arm.

"Are you sure? It's all right, I'll wait in the…"

"No, please stay." Cheri was sincere.

"She wants you to stay, so…" Dr. Cook gestured to the chair.

Tiffany patted Cheri's hand.

"I had several test done from your labs and from everything I've seen you are suffering from anemia."

"Every doctor I've seen has told me that," Cheri said sadly. "It's only been in the last few weeks that I've been losing weight again. I promise you, I've been trying to eat, even though I don't have an appetite."

"Well, that's not all. You also have a buildup of human chorionic gonadotopin in your system."

"What is that?"

Dr. Cook tilted her head to one side. "hCG is produced after implantation takes place and continues to increase until about the 12th week of pregnancy, so maybe you're experiencing some nausea?"

Tiffany gasped in surprise.

Cheri sat up straight from her slump position. "Are you saying.... I mean... are you sure?"

"Well, I suspected this when I was examining you. But I didn't want to say anything until I looked at all your test results and now that I have, the test only confirmed what I saw during your physical exam."

Cheri shut her eyes tightly as tears welled in them. She became so emotional that Tiffany put an arm around her shoulder in an attempt to consol her.

"But I haven't had a cycle in months." Cheri complained.

"If you hadn't been sexually active, you would have had one."

Tiffany leaned forward. "Is that why her appetite suddenly seem to have worsened making her lose weight again?" Tiffany asked.

"It could be. So, if you don't mind I want to do something different with you. I want you to try vegetarian meals. We're going to remove meats, fish, and any vegetable that has a strong taste to them. We'll do this for about four weeks. I'm putting you on prenatal vitamins and I want you to get plenty of rest. Can you do that?"

Cheri nodded several times. "Yes, no problem!"

"I want you to eat five small meals a day. If you get too nauseated, call me. I'm giving you my private number, because if you're not feeling well and Tiffany finds out, she's going to call me anyway."

"Yes, I am," Tiffany agreed.

Cheri was crying and laughing at the same time.

ഇഇരു

Cheri had been so excited that she totally forgot about Friday family movie night. As soon as she walked into the house, PJ grabbed her by the arm, rushing her to the theater. "Dad didn't want to start the movie until you got here. Where were you? We called the studio and your cell phone, we couldn't reach you!"

"I had an appointment."

"I ordered your favorite pizza. It came just before you got home so it's still hot."

Cheri stopped at the entrance of the room and gasped. "Your theater seats came!"

Preston smiled. "They look great, don't they?"

"Wonderful, I bet they're comfortable."

"Extremely."

"Now I understand why PJ is so excited."

"Well, movie night is his idea. He's been blowing up your cell phone. Where have you been?"

"I had an appointment with my new doctor." Cheri lowered her voice.

Preston really did not feel like hearing any depressing news so he quickly changed the subject. "I met with Pastor Wright and Deacon Roberts this afternoon."

"Yes, I remember you telling me you were meeting with them, how did it go?"

"Pastor Wright has decided not to resume as lead pastor."

"I see." Cheri dropped her gaze to the floor.

"I'll be installed as pastor, as long as you agree to it."

Cheri raised her head and stared at him for a moment. "I could never stop you from doing what is clearly your destiny."

Preston grasped her hand put it to his lips and kissed it. "I love you."

Cheri smiled. "I love you more."

"Your mother called. She was trying to reach you too."

"I forgot to turn my phone back on after my appointment."

"She told me to tell you that she and your father would be here on Wednesday and they're staying until after the reception."

"Their room is ready—and I'm actually getting excited about the reception."

"Well, I'm glad to hear that. Your parents have really put a lot of effort into making this a grand event."

"I know." Cheri agreed.

"Are we ready to start the movie?" PJ asked from the doorway.

"Where is my frozen drink?" Preston asked his son.

"And where is my pizza?" Cheri asked in wonderment.

Epilogue

The reception was a spectacular event. More than two hundred people had come to celebrate Cheri and Preston's union two years after their wedding day.

Pastor Wright, who was sitting at the head table, looked at the happy couple with a wide smile. This event was his first since his recuperation. He stood and tapped his glass, getting everyone's attention.

"I know I haven't known Pastor Preston and First Lady Cheri Owens as long as many of you have. However, we've shared a lot of time together. I know Preston and Cheri as being a loving and caring couple. I also know their history and as many of you now know... they certainly belong together." The audience applauded. "I'm now going to let Bishop Owens have the floor to address his son and his daughter-in-law."

Preston's father began slowly. "This evening's event was designed to bring two families together. And it's my opinion that both families have learned some real good lessons through all this."

He cleared his throat. "First of all, we must listen to our children. Let them have their say and then we'll be able to evaluate a dilemma objectively and honestly applying the Word of God to get the best result according to His will. We can pray, and not become part of the problem, but an advocate for the solution. There is a scripture that come to mind to support what I just said and it in Micah 6:8 and in part it says..."what does the Lord require of you, but to do justly, and to love mercy, and to walk humbly with your God?

"Number two, we've learned we can't pick our children's mate. Only God can do that and so what God has joined together no man can pull apart. Thirdly, we've learned to be forgiving. I know for a fact that I'm now quick to forgive. Forgiveness is due everyone that asks for it. After that, it's up to the receiver to accept it or reject it. According to God's law, as long as we ask with humility, it out of our hands and into the hands of the one we asked for forgiveness from. Even God forgives us when we say, I'm sorry, 'cause in Roman's tenth chapter and ninth verse it says, "That if thou shalt confess with thy mouth the Lord Jesus, and shalt believe in thine heart that God hath raised him from the dead, thou shalt be saved." By doing that simple directive I was able to save my soul and secure my future for eternity."

Bishop Owens wiped his brow and looked over to Cheri's mother. "Mrs. Anderson, I think this is a good place for you to finish up this speech."

Cheri's mother stood. "Thank you, Bishop Owens. I too learned what real forgiveness is. I lived for almost thirty years not forgiving my husband. And because I had no compassion or forgiveness in my heart, the years rolled by and I became a bitter old woman. My bitterness has not only hurt me but my oldest child and I believe it's the only reason she's not here today." Bernadette sniffled. "I'm praying for her and I'm showing her by example God's love. I found out that the only Bible some people will ever read is by watching you. An unforgiving spirit is a terrible thing. It's like poison. It will infect your very soul and cause you misery and pain that will affect you physically as well. So to do justly and to love mercy and walking humbly with God has been my intention so when anyone read me they see God in me.

"I read in the Bible that a man asked Jesus "Is it lawful for a man to put away his wife? tempting him. Mark 10:3-9 answered and said unto them, what did Moses command you? And they said, Moses suffered to write a bill of divorcement, and to put her away. And Jesus answered and said unto them, For the hardness of your heart he wrote you this precept. But from the beginning of the creation God made them male and female. For this cause shall a man leave his father and mother, and cleave to his wife; And they twain shall be one flesh: so then they are no more twain, but one flesh. What therefore God hath joined together, let not man put asunder."

She looked around her. "If we had listened to these two people before Preston married another woman, we would be celebrating their anniversary of many years of marriage instead of recognizing its start. When Cheri and Preston finally decided to follow their hearts, my daughter came to me and asked me a question. She said, "Mama, why should we suffer the rest of our lives for one mistake that can be corrected?" Now my answer is, you don't have to. Admit it, forgive it and move on."

She turned and faced the younger couple. "Preston and Cheri, be good to each other. Be quick to forgive and never go to sleep with an argument not settled. Love each other and please give me some grandbabies. You're gonna have to have them quickly because neither one of you are getting any younger." Laughter could be heard throughout the room.

"One can chase a thousand and two can put ten thousand to flight. All that's here today, be in prayer with me that God will bless Cheri's wound to be fruitful and multiply."

"Amen." Her father's voice rang out loudly.

Preston leaned over and whispered into Cheri's ear, "Want to tell them now?"

"No," She whispered her answer. "I'll let them figure it out on their own. In a few months I'll be thick enough around the waist for them to do just that!"

Dear Reader:

The ULTIMATE DILLEMMA: Forgive Me Lord was written during one of the most stressful times in my life. I lost both of my parents and a sister in Christ, Gloria Wheeler who was one of my proofreaders. Then to add to my grief, I found out I had thyroid cancer.

Immediately after I went into treatment I found myself deep in depression and with prayer, family and friends I was lifted from a sinking abyss. So, once I began writing again I sprinkled a little about depression in the storyline.

Though this story became more about Cheri, I pray I have covered enough about Preston so you would feel compassion for him and know that love covers a multitude of sin.

Like my last manuscript this story came out a lot different than I originally planned. But it is my hope that you have enjoyed this ride and waiting to catch the next dilemma which I've already begun to write called Tiffany's Dilemma: A Matter Of Time.

To those of you who have been writing me about Jason's story, though I haven't been inspired to write one as of yet doesn't mean it won't happen. And to everyone who think Theashia should have a story, I agree.

Your email and snail mail kept me going during so of the darkest time in my life. I thank you for each and every one of them. So please keep them coming.

Until next time, I pray God continues to bless and keep you.

Peace,

Reign

P.O. Box 4731
Rocky Mount, NC 27803-0731
On the Web: www.Reign.NickiAngela.net
Reign@NickiAngela.net

About The Author

Reign is a minister of the Gospel and the minister of music at New Revelations Baptist Church. Reign began writing at a very young age, however her gift for writing was not recognized in the beginning as an author of novels, but of lyrics set to music. Today, Reign's writing career is a very large part of her ministry. Reign lives with her husband and three of their six children in the Raleigh, North Carolina area.

Other Books In This Series

Book #1
Ivy's Dilemma: Thy Will Be Done
ISBN 978-0977093601

Book #2
Jade's Dilemma: Lead Us Not Into Temptation
ISBN 978-0977093656

Book #3
Sheena's Dilemma: It's Better To Marry Than To Burn
ISBN 978-0978897703